wings

Nicole Harman

.

WINGS

Copyright © 2020 by Nicole Harman.

Cover design by Cory DeYonker
ISBN: 978-1-7358940-0-3 (paperback)
ISBN: 978-1-7358940-1-0 (ebook)

To
All the friends and family who continue to encourage
me to write.

one

There comes a day when a person comes of age. It's a special time. Empowering almost. You would be looked at as the mature person you desired to be viewed as. You're included in more serious matters and conversations. Everything would change from that day on. It was the day a person got their wings. The wings that showed they had matured. The majestic beauties that gave a person access to all parts of Athra, both on ground and in the sky. These wings gave one an almost completed look. Each pair is entirely unique to the person. They just seem to fit their character in some way, as if they were always a part of them.

Take my mom, for example. She is a tall and thin woman, with a graceful way about her. No matter what she is doing, she always looks radiant and elegant. Her hair sleek and well tamed and the color of melted caramel. Her eyes are an icy blue color. When you look at her, you feel safe and welcomed. Her wings match the color of her eyes. The edges are straight and, yet, they look light and airy, almost like a beautiful silk fabric. They are simple in design, but when she flies, they glimmer in the light. It's almost as if they shine from somewhere within.

I, on the other hand, don't have my wings. Every day since I was small, I have wondered what it was like. I admired my mom and how her wings complimented her so well. I would imagine what mine would look like; how they would feel. Would they make me look as elegant as my mom's? Would they complement my coffee-colored eyes? Or maybe match the sun-kissed highlights in my wavy hair? Each day that passes is another day of wonder as I watch everyone I know show off their wings.

"Maybe today is the day!" Mom said as she greeted me in the kitchen with a homemade apple cinnamon muffin, complete with her sweet brown sugar crumble topping. She brushed a strand of long sandy blonde hair out of my face and kissed my forehead. I have heard her say this for almost a year now. Every day, the same morning greeting. As always, I smiled and took the muffin from her.

My older brother came bursting through the back door of our small house. He was grinning from ear to ear. His messy blonde hair fell in his face for only a moment before his masculine hand brushed it to the side out of habit. His bare arms gleamed of sweat. *He must have been out wing racing with his friends again.*

He turned to shut the door. "Have you heard? The Clayton boy got his wings today!" He informed with joy.

I allowed my gaze to fall on his wings. They were sturdy and of petrified wood. The lines were bold and defined, and they were a deep brown in color.

"That's wonderful," Mom said happily.

My heart sank. The Clayton boy was over a year younger than I am. He was the last of his age class to get his wings.

"So, it's time to catch up, sis!" Teased my brother as he joined me for a muffin at the table.

"Bray, that's enough," Mom cooed at him. "You know she can't do anything about it. Don't worry, Esmari. They'll come."

He was right, though; it was time to catch up. Not having my wings yet was almost unheard of. When someone was this late in getting their wings, it usually meant that they weren't going to get them at all. There was only one case of that happening in our area, and only a handful of cases from other towns where someone didn't ever get their wings.

What if I am one of the few whose wings never come?

Just the thought of that gave me chills. I would never be able to race my classmates. I would never be able to visit Sky Athra myself. I wouldn't be allowed to advance in schooling much longer, either. A lot of jobs require one to have wings, so my options there would be limited, too. As much as I hate it, I would need to really start to explore what it would be like without wings.

Bray, who had long finished his muffin by now, got up with a jolt, scaring me out of my thoughts. "Welp, I'm off to classes!" he said with a grin. Ever since he entered into higher schooling, the one you need wings to attend, he was excited to learn.

"See ya later," I said, waving him goodbye. Was I jealous of him? Sure, just a little. But he's still my brother, and I was still happy for him.

"Oh, will dad be back today?" Bray asked. Our dad had been traveling with some of his friends visiting a neighbor town to exchange some goods from our town's businesses.

"He should be returning tomorrow. Now, get going before you're late!" Mom shooed. He closed the door behind him, and Mom and I were left in a long awkward silence. Mom turned to me with a warm smile. "You had better get going to your classes, too. I don't want you to be late."

"Would it be okay if I go to Ruby's after class?" I blurted out. I didn't realize what I was even asking before I asked it.

I must have caught Mom off guard as much as me. She paused and let her surprised face settle into a calm expression. I hadn't seen Ruby in a while. She was this very nice lady who lived on the edge of town. She always kept to herself and didn't ask for anything. She was also the only person who never got her wings. Mom and I occasionally go to visit with her over a cup of tea. She always would tell us we were welcome anytime.

"Sure," Mom said in such a way that I knew she understood why I needed to go. I think almost more than I did. I wanted to know how to do life without wings. As much as Mom believed that I would get my wings still, I needed an idea of a plan if that never happened. Mom handed me two muffins and sent me off to school.

Outside, the morning air was crisp. Athra was beautiful. The massive trees were in full bloom and shaded the red dirt path that led to the school. Most of my classmates fluttered by me. Hunter met me at the third tree, just like always. Even though he had his wings, he always walked with me. His jet-black hair was perfectly styled, as usual, and even with the morning breeze, it didn't budge. He pulled a hand out of his pant pocket and waved at me.

"Here," I said, handing him one of Mom's muffins.

His hazel eyes sparkled and a giddy grin stretched across his mouth as he snatched the muffin out of my hand. He brought it up to his nose and took a big whiff.

"Your mom is seriously the best!" he praised. I rolled my eyes as I watched him slowly start to eat the muffin, savoring each bite.

We made our way up the path until we reached the rusty gates of the school. The school was small and rather simplistic. Nothing more than a couple of classrooms containing chairs and desks and chalkboards at the front. The walls of the classroom were bland. Just a dirty tan color accompanied by the only hint of vibrancy in the room, provided by a couple of pretty nature pictures our teacher put up. But Mr. Clove had enough personality to bring any boring space to life. He had a way of teaching that was anything but basic. Quirky, yet informative. A bit on the eccentric side at times, but it's enjoyable. He believed that you needed to smile in a classroom.

Today, Mr. Clove had our desks off to one side, and our chairs placed in the middle of the room. He was always changing the room up to "keep us on our toes." Hunter and I took seats off to the side and settled in. Mr. Clove took his place toward the chalkboard to begin the class. He didn't say a word, just picked up a piece of chalk and began writing on the board slowly and dramatically. The chatter from fellow students quieted. When he was finished, he peeked over his shoulder, and made an over-exaggerated turn to face us. He widened his eyes and made a ridiculous, sarcastically serious face. Hunter and I looked at each other and giggled. *This is going to be a good lesson.*

He stepped aside to reveal what he wrote on the board. "Royals."

"Alright, today we are going to be talking about the history of our Royals," he said, dropping his silly expression. His frizzy brown hair flopped around on his head while he talked. He stuck one hand in his pocket and fidgeted with the chalk in the other. "Our Royals are just what they sound like, Royalty. But they don't just get born into it; they all are chosen, in sorts, by some defining factor that only they know about. A Royal can be from any town, but here in Athra, there has never been a Royal chosen. These Royals are trained to keep peace and order among the towns. They keep us safe. Royals have been around for hundreds of years, and they usually don't travel much to the smaller towns. In fact, it has been about fifteen years since one of the Royals, or any of their accompanying, has visited here. Some of you might remember the festival we put on when the Royal was here, but they only appeared briefly at the festival, making it to where only a few people in our town really even saw them. Royals are rumored to have only ever been women, but their accompanying can be either men or women. It is also said that only women can possess the 'power' that is needed, though no one other than the Royals know what that power is or if that is even true. Their secrecy is both intriguing and understandable. They are not meant to be big and famous. But, rather, just a part of the lands in their own way; almost like a long-lost legend."

Mr. Clove took a stack of paper in his hand that before held the chalk, all the while leaving his other hand in his pocket. His blue eyes twinkled as he instructed, and his wings that looked of handmade paper lay calm down his back as if they had fallen asleep to his own teaching. He gave the stack of paper to a student and motioned for them to pass it around.

"For the remainder of class, I would like you all to write—" moans of disgust came from students all around the classroom, including from Hunter beside me. I gave him a shove with my elbow. "If you all are finished," he raised his eyebrow and glanced around the room as he waited for the class to hush. "As I was saying, I would like you to write out answers to the following questions." He picked up the piece of chalk again and wrote out his questions on the board as he spoke. "If you could spend a day with a Royal, what would you do? What would you want to ask them about? Where would you go with them?" Mr. Clove set down the piece of chalk and began to wander around the room. "I would like at the least a full paragraph answering these questions. You can make it into a story, or you can just flat-out answer. Either way, you need to turn it in to me before leaving class."

He took a seat in his chair up toward the front of the room. After some pencils were passed around, we were ready for the assignment. Some of the students sat on the floor and began to write, while others, like myself, took advantage of being close to one of the desks on the sides of the room and pulled our chairs up to them. I got comfy and lifted my pencil to my paper and—

Nothing.

I was stumped. It's not that I don't have anything to write, but quite the opposite. I didn't know where to begin. I had so many ideas of things I would ask, places I would want to experience with them, people I would want to share the entire experience with...

That's where I should begin! Who would I want to share the experience with first? My mom to start. And I would want to enjoy a pressure-free conversation over one of my mom's homemade muffins. I would ask about everything I could. How do they know who the chosen Royal is? What if the chosen isn't who they thought? I would want to know about their daily tasks, and how they keep order with everyone and everything. I want to know about what they do for fun, and if wings are required for all of it. If they look down on those without wings. What are the so-called "powers" that they possess, and what are they for? I would want to see where they live, what it's like to be in their shoes.

I was writing away and so lost in my thoughts that when I finished, I looked up to find that I was one of the last in the room. Even Hunter had ditched me. I got up and presented my paper and pencil to Mr. Clove.

"Glad to see that you got into this assignment, Esmari. I hope you have a good summer break. See you in a couple months for fall classes." He smiled.

I thanked him and left the classroom. Hunter was waiting just outside the door for me. We walked together, chatting and laughing until we got well into the center of town. There was so much commotion, as usual in this part. So many places to be, and things to see and do. We walked by a café; as the delicious aroma caught our attention, Hunter and I gawked at the food through the window, glued to the view as we passed. Beautiful music came from some wind chimes as the breeze touched them in the "Whatnot's" store across the way. I found myself mesmerized by the items in the window of the "Things for Wings" clothing and accessories store. Hunter yanked me away from the window and back into reality. High above, people flew to Sky Athra, their shadows dancing on the dirt below. I always loved to watch and imagine how glamorous it must be to experience it all up there. Hunter disappeared into a shop, and I sat on a bench admiring the bustle of the town. He came back with two small ice cream cones of our favorite flavor, Barely Berry, vanilla bean ice cream with huckleberry swirl. I snatched it and raised an eyebrow as if to ask how he came of these.

"I know a guy," he said in a sly tone and took a very serious lick of his treat, just before he snorted and sent us both into a roaring fit of laughter.

We sat at the bench outside the door of the shop. Savoring every drip of the delicious ice cream, we played a game trying to guess which store each person was going to, keeping score in the dirt with a nearby stick. As usual, Hunter was winning. Since he ran a lot of errands for his parents, who owned the fabric and tailoring shop, he knew many of the townspeople and their habits and needs. He had a lot of connections, too, and was always helping people out with the slightly selfish intent that he will get something in return. When he had sufficiently beat me at our made-up game, and we had finished our treats, we decided it was time to get going again, making our way to his parents' shop. After some small talk with his parents, we parted ways.

I made it to the edge of town in a complete daze. Before I knew it, I was opening the dazzling gray painted gate that enclosed Ruby's yard. She had a little pathway, just barely wide enough to walk on leading up to her front door. To either side, leaves from wildflowers and tall grasses grew together. She had her own humble sanctuary out her front door, including a porch chair sitting right out in the middle of her yard under the shade of a large oak tree. Her house was simple but welcoming. The windows were wide open as they always were on warm days. I could see her sitting at her small table, working away at something.

"Hi, Ruby!" I called out to her as I came up to the house.

"Oh!" she said, looking out at me. "Hello, dear! Come on in, I'll put some tea on."

I reached out to the brass handle of her newly painted teal door, opened it, and entered her house. It was quaint, nothing too extravagant, but had lots of personality. Next to the front door was a small black table holding a vase full of flowers from her yard. As I walked into her front room, I was greeted by the familiar sound of creaky wooden floorboards. Her house smelled fresh. A large bookcase to one side of the room was only half full, while the remainder of the books were stacked in little piles all around on the floor. I took a glance at the table where Ruby was before I walked in, to see little notes scribbled on a paper sitting next to two open books.

"Sorry! I was in the middle of reorganizing the bookshelf when I came across a book I forgot I had," Ruby fussed as she shuffled the books off the table. She plopped them on the floor and gave a satisfied nod with her decision of placement. Her long purple skirt swished against the ground. I sat down in one of her old white chairs by the table. The kettle whistled on the stove, and she hurried into her small kitchen around the corner. "Where are we heading today? To the tropics or the woods?" she asked.

"Seems like a good day for the tropics," I replied, excited to see what kind of fruity tea she had in store for us today. Ruby came around the corner with a tray holding two unmatched teacups, a steaming tea kettle, some sugar, and a plate full of assorted snacks. She set it down at the table and smoothed her skirt before taking a seat at the table with me. Her face was kind, and there was this sparkle in her eye whenever she had company. Her bright red hair was pinned back into a messy bun. She was like me, average in size and basic looking. But she had this warmth about her personality that drew you in. And she was interesting to talk to, always having something new to bring to a conversation.

"So, Esmari," Ruby said as she poured a cup of tea for the both of us. "What's the topic for today?"

"Is it that obvious?" I asked. She always did know when I came with a motive. She just smiled and handed me my tea. We took a great big whiff of the aroma coming from our cups. My nose was met by warm smells of sweet citrus. I took a sip and began again. "Well, I wanted to know what it's like to go through life without wings."

"Oh, my! You really just came out with it! And that's quite a topic!" She exclaimed with a smile. "But you already know what it's like to not have wings. I think you want to know what it's like to never get your wings. What it's like the day you realize they are never coming. That's the real questions you are intending to ask."

"Yeah, I guess you're right," I said in thought.

Ruby took a sip of her tea and sighed. "Well, I'm not going to sugar coat it, Miss Esmari. It's hard. To watch your friends grow into their wings. To soar, literally," she laughed for a moment, "sorry couldn't help myself with that pun. But you know what, one day I just realized that I was going to succeed in my own way. Sure, I can't go to Sky Athra. But I have everything I have ever needed down here."

"How did you know you were never getting your wings? I mean—" I paused, looking for the right words to ask. "Did it just never happen, or did you just know?"

Ruby's eyes grew soft as she looked me over. "I had this gut feeling one day. Of a sense of emptiness—" she began. She tapped the ring on her finger against the cup in a thinking manner.

"I'm so sorry," I muttered.

"No, no! It wasn't all that bad. I mean, sure, I felt emptiness. But there was also this bit of relief. Like, I no longer was waiting on this big event to come. I no longer had to plan my days waiting on my wings. I was able to just actually start to move forward. I was the talk of the town too!" She laughed as she sat up tall and proud. "I had never been so popular. I had my whole life in front of me, and no one could tell me how to live it because no one knew how to! It was invigorating! I could try anything I wanted. Which I'm sure is how a lot of people feel after they get their wings, now that I think about it."

"When did you know?" I asked as I took another sip of my tea.

"Well, I guess I always had this sort of — I don't know — a feeling? And one day it became clearer and clearer. I think in the same way that people get their wings, I got the knowing that mine wouldn't come. But I knew when I was just about your age. My parents were a bit sadder than I was, I think. They had such high hopes and dreams for what they wanted my life to be. And for a long time, I think they were embarrassed that they didn't have a child who would amount to much in this society. But I didn't actually care. I was enjoying not having anyone expect anything of me!" Ruby explained. Talking to her made me feel so at ease.

"I think I am just wondering where my wings are. I don't feel like they aren't coming necessarily. I guess, I just don't know what I feel." I swirled the remainder of the tea around in my cup as I talked.

"Trust me, Esmari, you would know that your wings aren't ever coming. And if you just don't have that feeling, then your wings are just taking their sweet time to come to you. I think we will see them very, very soon." She winked at me. "I would bet my tea on it." I giggled and snagged a little cookie off the tray.

We enjoyed lighter conversation for quite a while, and I helped with some of her book organizing. She told me she was always switching around things in her house because, as she would say, it forced her attention on things left in the dark for too long. Eventually, she and I both realized how late in the day it was getting. She invited me to accompany her to Hunter's parent's shop.

"I wanted to make a trip to the shop before the day is over. I am in need of a new skirt and could always use your opinion on the fabric!" she said in a song-like manner as she delivered our teacups to the sink.

"That sounds like fun!" I said, accepting her invitation.

She and I closed up her house and made our way down the path to the shops. The air was filled with a sweet smell coming from the cafe where they were making pies. I watched as townspeople flew above us. I could see the faintest glimmer of pink and blue lights coming from one of the buildings up there. *I wonder what it looks like to look down at everyone down here from way up in the sky?* Ruby noticed me gazing up at the sky and gave my shoulders a quick squeeze.

"You'll be up there soon. I just know it." She smiled.

We entered the fabric shop and were greeted by the jingle of the bell on the door. Colored fabric of every pattern and every color one could imagine filled the walls. The shop was well lit and had brick flooring. There was a large table right in the center of the shop with rulers and scissors and scraps of recently trimmed fabric. I ran my hand across the fuzzy pink fabric in the discount bin and took a deep breath in. The familiar scent of oranges and freshly washed sheets filled my nose and brought a smile to my face.

"Hello, ladies," Hunter greeted with a silly smirk on his face as if trying to be alluring. "How may we help you today?"

"You're so weird sometimes." I laughed.

"Hunter, don't scare our customers away."

Hunter's dad teased as he joined us. "Hello, Ruby and Esmari. What brings us in today?"

"Hello, Cameron. I am in need of a new skirt," Ruby said.

"Well, you came at a great time! We just dyed some new fabric that would be perfect for that! Now let's see—" Hunter's dad informed as he glanced around the shop. "It's around here somewhere. Ah! Here we are!" He pulled a beautiful deep teal gradient fabric.

"What do you think Esmari?" Ruby asked as we felt the soft fabric.

"I think it's perfect. And I don't believe I have seen you in this color much." I approved.

"You are right! But I don't know if I have tops to go with, so I will need you to make me something to match it too," she stated. She and Cameron stepped off to the side to verify measurements and discuss pricing, leaving Hunter and me to chat a bit.

Ruby finished her purchase and was on her way shortly after. Hunter's dad found odds and ends for us to help with while we hung out. I enjoyed simple afternoons like this, spending time with him. We spent most of the time laughing or goofing around. Hunter's dad showed us how they created adaptable tops for people with or without wings or would have us try our hand at a few stitches here and there. There was just something about the feeling in the breeze that would waft through the shop when the door would open. It was that feeling that makes you feel special. Time seemed to slow down for a moment as I took that special feeling in. I felt it all the way to my toes. That feeling of security and purity of the moment.

two

Sometime in the middle of that night, I woke up abruptly. Something wasn't right. I didn't know what. I was too dazed to really put my finger on it. Getting my bearings, I sat up in bed and rubbed my eyes. The cool night air seeped in through my window, tossing the curtains from side to side in a sort of slow dance. The moon was beautifully bright tonight, I noted. I took a deep breath in. Something pulled at the skin on my back. My blanket fell off of me, and I shivered. Everything hurt. What was going on? Slowly, I lowered myself back down onto my soft bed and closed my eyes.

I dozed off thinking of all of the beautiful fabrics from Hunter's family's shop. The multitude of colors danced around my head. I remembered how soft some had felt against my hands. A dark iridescent fabric caught my eye. It glimmered all different colors in the warm light of the shop. All I could hear was the sound of my own breath breathing in and out... in and out... My hand was reaching out for the fabric, but it seemed like my arm wasn't long enough to touch it. I stretched, and stretched, and stretched, and with the tip of my finger, I dusted the edge of it. Suddenly, it burst into flames. I looked around, and everything was on fire. It was getting so hot. I tried to get out, but there was no door. Just flames everywhere. I tried to take a breath, but I couldn't, the air was too thin.

I jolted awake, gasping for air. I felt so hot. My skin burned. Tears started streaming down my face. My body hurt so badly. Why did my room feel so much larger, and I felt so much more alone than ever? I tried calling out for help, but my mouth was so parched that nearly no sound came out. I was scared. *What is happening to me?* Again, I called out. Somehow, I managed to make a sound. I don't even know what I said. My ears were ringing so much. *Make it stop!* I squeezed my eyes shut.

"Esmari," said a voice.

I opened my eyes and saw my brother standing over me. I was trembling. I opened my mouth, wanting to say something. I was at a loss for words. My head felt so jumbled.

"Hey, it's okay," he cooed. "Mom's coming," he was keeping a calm voice, but I could tell he was concerned.

My mom came into the room and began gently wiping me down with a cool, damp cloth. I searched her face for answers. Her eyebrows were pulled together with worry. She just kept softly wiping me down.

"It wasn't like this when I got mine," whispered Bray to mom.

"It's different for everyone, sweetie," she responded. There was a slight tremble in her voice.

"This doesn't seem right," Bray mumbled under his wavering breath as he smoothed my hair.

"Can you fetch her something to drink? She is getting dehydrated." Mom asked. I could tell she was just wanting to protect him.

The room was spinning. I couldn't focus on much. Even though I could feel Mom's touch, she sounded muffled as if she was in another room. The ringing in my ears would get louder and quieter. Bray said something about when he got his. *His what?* It donned on me. *His wings? Was I finally getting mine? Was it supposed to feel like this?* Another wave of fire rushed over me. I bit my lip.

"Here, take a sip, sis." Bray held a cup to my mouth. I took just enough to wet my throat. I was afraid of getting sick.

I looked up at him through my teary eyes. "Wings—" I squeaked out. I intended it to be a full question but couldn't fathom more than a word.

He managed a smile and nodded. "Yeah, sis, wings."

Just then, another burning wave spread through my body. I blinked quickly. There were stars everywhere. I could barely hear. Mom was trying to say something. I tried reading her lips. It was so muffled. Everything began to get darker and darker. There was a whooshing sound in my head now too.

———

I could hear someone talking, but I couldn't understand what they were saying. They were out in the hallway, that much I could tell. I opened my eyes to see a pink glow covering my room. Was it daytime already? Bray met eyes with me and came into the room. He lifted a cup to my lips. They felt so chapped. I took a few small sips of water and laid my head back down. I shivered. I felt like ice. It hurt to shiver. I winced. Bray pulled my blankets over me and tucked them around me like mom and dad used to when we were little. I was so tired.

"Bray—" I managed to squeak out through my chattering teeth.

"Close your eyes. Just rest," Bray said softly.

———

A comforting warmth from the sun coming in through my window fell on my cheek. I could hear someone shift near me in the room. Slowly, I opened my eyes and let my gaze search the space before me. My room was filled with a golden glow. What time was it? I felt groggy and worn out. My blankets were on the ground, and all that covered me was a thin sheet. The world sounded so quiet, and yet the silence was so loud. Why was that? *Oh! The ringing in my ears stopped!* I felt so different. I tried to remember what happened. A sound in the corner of the room caught me off guard.

"Dad?" I said softly. His eyes met mine, and his face lit up with a huge grin. He set down the book he had in his hands and came over to me.

"Well, now there's my sweet girl," he said. His voice was just as raspy as always, but so nice to hear. He felt my forehead with the back of his hand. "How are you feeling?"

"I'm not sure. A little sore, I think. And still waking up, I suppose," I told him. My mouth was dry again. My stomach growled.

"You're hungry, too, I guess." He chuckled. "I'll be back."

He started for the door. The grays in his deep brown hair glistened in the light. He held himself with dignity. The trip really did his spirit well and added a little extra pep in his step, as it usually did.

"Dad, wait. When did you get back?" I asked. My whole timeline felt muddled together.

"Got back yesterday mornin', which was a day later than I planned, due to the multitude of goods we weren't anticipating on bringing back. Your poor mother was having to worry about the both of us." He shook his head with a smirk on his face. "You've been in and out of it for days." He slipped out the door.

Days? How could it have been days? I thought maybe hours, but *days*? I felt like I was just at Ruby's house. If this started that night, dad was due home the following day. But he said it took him an extra day to get back, and he got back yesterday… This was going on for three days? That couldn't be right, could it? I had lost all that time? My stomach growled again. When was the last time I ate? A vague memory of the taste of a salty cracker came to mind, but when was that? A feeling of overwhelm washed over me. I was beginning to feel scared. I sat up and felt a weight pulling at my back. *My wings.*

It seemed such an unnatural thought to have. I had spent so much time anticipating them and ultimately just feeling like they would never come. But yet, here they were, on my back. I wanted so badly to see them, but at the same time, I was afraid to. What would they be like? I didn't try to turn my head to look at them. I wanted to see them in full, all at once, in a mirror. But, at the same time, I enjoyed this time of mystery. Just taking in how it felt to have them on my back. They seemed to have found their way through the custom discrete openings in my shirt back. That's good. I shifted my weight as I sat and observed how the new weight was distributing itself. They felt weird and bulky. That was going to take some time to get used to.

"I have wings," I whispered to myself. It even felt foreign to say. I didn't know whether to laugh or cry or what.

Dad reentered the room with a plate of fruit and one of Mom's muffins, his wavy hair bouncing as he walked. Mom followed at his heels. There was something about their eyes that was almost proud. Not that I really did anything, but I'm sure it was for the coming of age. I felt different in a way, yet exactly the same. But at the moment, all I could really focus on was how good the food looked. They handed me the plate, and I dug in immediately. The taste of the fruit caught me off guard. It was sweeter, more intense. My mouth was so packed with flavor! Unlike it had ever been before. *Was this normal? Was this my new normal?*

"Are you alright, sweetie?" Mom asked as she searched my face for answers of why I had paused from eating.

"The food tastes different than before," I remarked.

"Oh, that's just your imagination, Esmari." Dad laughed. "It's the same as it has always been."

Was it, though? Was I just expecting everything to be different now that I had wings? I took another bite and analyzed as I chewed. *No. I'm not imagining it. It tastes different.* Maybe this wasn't something that they experienced, but all I knew is I wanted more. Food had never tasted so delicious! It was like I was rediscovering the fruits as I ate. I wanted to savor their flavor, their texture against my tongue, their complexity that I had never appreciated before. Before I knew it, I had finished eating my food.

I adjusted myself and was caught off guard by the pulling sensation on my back. Definitely something that was going to take some getting used to. I wanted to ask so many questions, yet at the same time, I wanted to discover everything for myself. A moment of anxious excitement washed over me, sending chills all the way down to my toes. I don't know how to have wings. I mean, I was so used to *not* having wings that I never thought I would have to learn, yet here I was. *How do I not bump into stuff with them? How do I change clothes? Does it just come naturally, or is it an awkward transition?*

"Do you want to see them?" Bray asked. I didn't even notice him enter the room. I felt hot in the face. I was scared. *Why am I scared?*

After a long pause, or so it felt in my head, I answered with a wary smile. "Of course I want to see them!"

Mom and Dad helped me up from the bed and held onto my arms until I wasn't wobbly anymore. My palms were sweaty. *What if they are ugly? What if I don't like them? What if they didn't suit me well? Was that a thing? Would people make fun of me because of them? No, they had to be happy for me, right?*

"Close your eyes," Bray said, taking my arm. "I want it to be like a grand reveal!" He led me gently over to the mirror against the wall. My heart was pounding. I tried to catch my breath. "Okay, open your eyes."

I took one big deep breath and opened my eyes up. My hair was a mess, and my clothes were wrinkled from being in bed for so long. But I found that I didn't care. There they were. My wings, attached to my back.

They were black as night with a satin shine to them. But all through them, they looked like they were cracked. Almost like broken black glass. The top and bottom sides were smooth, however, the sides furthest from my spine were uneven and looked sharp. I lifted my hands to feel them. They felt like thin tulle fabric, yet strong. The uneven edges were far from sharp; they were soft like a feather. They seemed small to me. Almost half the size of everyone in my family. I turned back and forth, admiring them from both sides. The right wing and left wing weren't even the same size. Something caught my eye. A shimmer. I swayed again, trying to determine where it came from. At the bottom of my left wing, close to my shoulder blade, there was a small metallic copper smear, almost like someone touched me with paint on their pinky finger. They looked strange on me.

"Whoa!" Hunter breathed. He was suddenly in my doorway, his eyes wide. "I came by to see if you were finally up, and, uh, whoa—"

I smiled at my friend. It was so nice to see him. I looked at my mom, who had tears in her eyes, holding on to my dad's hand. She gently dabbed the tears from streaming down her cheeks and rested her head on Dad's shoulder. Bray, who was standing tall with his arms folded, smirked at me. I waited for him to tease me or say something silly. He didn't. Maybe because he wanted me to enjoy taking it all in, like he had. I felt odd with them all just staring at me.

"Okay, already," I said sheepishly.

Mom ticked her tongue. Smiling, she shook her head at me. "My Esmari with her wings," she said softly.

"Mom," I said, embarrassed.

"We will leave you two to catch up," Dad said, starting to pull Mom away.

"I just want to—" she said, lingering for another moment.

"Come on, love," Dad persuaded. "Thanks for coming, Hunter. Let us know if you need something."

Dad led Mom and Bray out, leaving Hunter and me to our thoughts. There was this moment of comfortable silence where we just took everything in. He joined me by the mirror and looked over my wings. Hunter touched them lightly with his fingertips, examining the details. I searched his face for any indications of what he really thought. I wanted his approval, but, at the same time, I wanted him to tell me he thought that they looked odd on me, too. I searched my own face and its features. The only thing that seemed to match and feel out of place all at once was the smear of copper on my wings. I guess it did match my eyes, in a way.

"Alright," I sighed. "Let me have it. Your raw, honest, unfiltered thoughts."

"They are pretty cool, I guess," Hunter said, rolling his eyes dramatically. I shoved him playfully. "Hey! Okay, okay. But, really, they are so different. And striking. They look out of place on you, but just because I have never seen you with wings. But they suit you. In some way."

"I don't know, I mean. They are *so* striking. So bold. That's not entirely me. And they are smaller than most people's wings. What if they don't carry me correctly? And the copper smear looks like something messed up. Like the whole wing was supposed to be that color, but it's not—" I rambled.

"Wait," Hunter interrupted. "What copper smear? They just look black to me."

"What do you mean? It's right there!" I said, pointing to it. It was rather small, but how could you miss the contrast in color?

Hunter just shrugged. He went to sit on my bed, and, before long, we were just talking about all kinds of different things. He was informing me and teaching me different things to do with my wings. Like, how to care for them. And how to maneuver with them, although we both agreed, I may have a better time with mine, being that they were smaller. That was actually something I found to be grateful for. That they were small so they would be less noticeable. But something in me was almost urging me to try this new style out. Almost.

"Well, you want to see what those things can do?" Hunter said.

three

I managed a rather ungraceful, and yet very needed shower, and after a safety talk from Mom, Hunter and I made our way outside. We went for a short walk to an open area, away from trees, houses, and anything else that I could possibly crash into. Hunter was so giddy about my wings, talking about all the fun we were going to have together. I think he was more excited than I was. He showed me how to open my wings up and tuck them behind me carefully. I almost hit him a few times. He taught me the basics of how my wings needed to be positioned to be able to begin my liftoff. We also talked about the different necessary precautions I needed to take to ensure my safety, as well as others who may be around me. And then the real fun began, learning how to fly.

I had an idea in my head how it was going to go. I would just flitter my wings and get a little height and glide gracefully around like I have seen so many others do. I would soar up high with a smooth swoop and then dive back down to the ground. All I needed to do was open my wings up, think what I wanted to do, and they would just do all the work. But now that I was about to fly, my wings felt bulky and foreign, like I didn't, couldn't, control them completely. It was an odd sensation.

"Okay, so, just watch me, and try to do what I do!" Hunter said.

He opened his wings up, and I realized it was the first time I really saw his wings. He usually kept them tucked away around me. They were perfectly symmetrical and a beautiful, perfectly even tone of jade. I admired them for a moment as he fluttered just above the ground.

"Well, aren't you coming?" he chimed, interrupting my thoughts.

Okay, Esmari, you can do this. Simple. Just open your wings and —

I flittered my wings just a little. My feet left the ground. I felt unstable, unable to keep from rocking back and forth. I watched as Hunter glided forward a few feet. I tried to get stable, and, once I was as stable as I could be, I attempted the same. However, instead of gliding oh, so gracefully, I jerked forward, crashing into Hunter and sending both of us into the ground. It took me a second to get my bearings. *This is way harder than I thought.* Hunter moaned under me.

"Oh! I am so so so sorry!" I exclaimed, realizing I was sitting on top of him. "Are you okay?"

"You are really terrible at this," he said, cracking a smile and squinting at me with one eye.

"Hey! Well, I blame the teacher!" I said snootily as I got back on my feet. I brushed off a puff of red dust and helped Hunter to his feet. He took a large, dramatic step back, sending us both into a laughing fit.

"Was this hard for you to learn?" I asked after we could catch our breath.

"Well, I guess it wasn't the smoothest at first. But it will get better. You just have to get to know your wings and really feel them, ya know?" he said.

It made me feel better, and not, all at once. I tried to really focus on my wings. Feel them, I guess. But even though they were right there, it still felt like they weren't all there. *I just need to learn them.* We tried again, and this time it felt a bit rocky but better as I hovered. I went to glide forward and —

CRASH! I flew backward and fell on to the ground.

"You gotta think about going forward and really feel your wings bring you forward," Hunter stated.

"I did, but they didn't obey, I guess," I sighed.

"It's okay! Try again! Third time's the charm!" Hunter called, still hovering in the air.

Okay. This time for sure. I closed my eyes and took a deep breath in. I thought of just my wings. I looked them over in my mind. I felt how they attached to my back. I opened my eyes and got ready to try again. I hovered just a few inches above the ground. I felt stable this time. Not perfectly, but better than before. I took another deep breath. And then, just like that, I glided forward to Hunter. I felt a surge through my wings. Suddenly, I felt connected with my wings, like they were understanding my commands. His face lit up with excitement.

"You did it!" he praised.

I felt so proud. Like I could do anything, go anywhere! I flew high up in the sky and dove back down. The sensation of the air against the edges of my wings sent chills down my spine. It was nothing like I imagined it would feel. This feeling of freedom engulfed every inch of me. I circled Hunter a few times, giggling as I did so.

"Woo!" I exclaimed.

"Whoa! You caught on fast!" Hunter said.

"It's like my wings are listening to me! This is so great!" I called to him, soaring up into the sky again. It was such a rush!

"What do you mean, 'listening to you?' You just have to control them like you would a limb. You are crazy sometimes!" Hunter called back.

I paused. I didn't feel like I was controlling a limb. It was different. I felt like I was working with my wings, and them with me. We were understanding each other. *Okay, that sounds a little crazy.*

My mind went blank. The sounds around me disappeared. And suddenly, a whisper echoed in my ears. "There," it said. It was a woman's voice; one I didn't recognize. It was gentle yet wise. And just as quickly as it came, it was gone, and I was aware of the sounds surrounding me. I shook my head and looked down at Hunter, who was coming up to join me. He seemed unfazed. Had he not heard it too? *Maybe he was too low to hear it.*

"You good?" he asked as he caught up with me. "You seemed to zone out for a second."

"Uh—" *Did I? Should I tell him? What was there to tell?* "Yeah, I'm just taking it all in." I gave him a quick smile.

"Oh, yeah. It's so cool seeing everything from up here. A new perspective," he said, waving his hands out in a grand gesture. "Kind of cool to be able to see the top of people's heads!"

Goofball. I rolled my eyes at him.

"How about a race? Since you seem to have a good handle on your wings!" Hunter grinned.

"Where to, kind sir?" I said in a majestic manner.

"The rules are as follows," he said, straightening his body and puffing out his chest in a tough, intimidating way. "First winged individual to touch that tree," he pointed off in the distance, "shall be declared the champion. On your marks! Get set! Go!"

Off we raced. I felt my wings slicing through the cool breeze. I zoned in on the tree. I could feel myself going faster and faster. Everything was zooming by me. I could hear the wind whistling in my ears, and a bird somewhere nearby chirping as if to cheer us on. My hair swirled behind me, gently brushing against my flapping wings. I focused on the tree, the finishing line. The leaves seemed to sway with the breeze. I didn't want this rush of adrenaline to end. And then, for a moment, everything seemed to slow down. A leaf on the tree broke off, and I could see each vein on it as it floated to the ground below. The sounds around me grew softer and slower. I could hear each of my wings cutting into the air in their own way, the right one almost a little louder than the other. I could smell the sweet aroma of the flowers below me and the slightly citrusy smell that always lingered on Hunter's clothes.

I blinked and suddenly realized the finish was upon me. I reached out and touched the tree. The bark was smooth like velvet with lots of grooves. My feet met the ground again, a familiar feeling that I welcomed. I looked around for Hunter, only to find him just barely fluttering to the tree.

"What in the world! That was—was—" He stammered with excitement and confusion.

"Exhilarating!" I exclaimed. I couldn't get over the incredible feeling. I wanted it back. I wanted to savor it forever.

"That was —wild!" He seemed to have made up his mind on the word he was looking for. "I mean, I shouted go, and off you went!"

"That's what you are supposed to do in races, Hunter!" I teased cheekily.

"Well, yeah, I know that. But you really just went! It was like one second you were beside me, and the next, you were way in front of me! And the way you moved, with such precision. It was just— just— wow!" Hunter rambled like he was in his own world, waving his arms around as he talked.

As he went on, exhaustion washed over me. I was hungry and tired, yet excited still about wanting to explore the world with my new wings. I wanted to see Sky Athra. I wanted to fly more. I wanted to fly as fast as I could again. But I felt like I could barely stand anymore, which frustrated me more than anything. *I just slept for days, how could I possibly be this tired?*

"You okay, Es?" Hunter asked, suddenly snapping out of his ranting. "You look like you could fall over. I suppose you are probably a bit tired from your first flight." Hunter put his arm around my shoulders. I felt heavy, and I leaned into his sturdy stature.

"I guess I'm just a bit worn out," I whispered. I couldn't stand anymore. My legs gave out. There was an odd sensation deep inside me. A feeling I couldn't quite describe.

"Whoa!" Hunter gasped as he caught me and lowered both of us to the ground. It was dusty and warm. I felt each grain of sand against my hand so vividly. "Okay—uh—well—I guess we will just hang here until you are good." Hunter's voice sounded wary.

I could hear someone's shoes grinding against the coarse sand nearby, walking toward us. My surroundings were fading away. *Tall, bulky build, male.* I could almost see the figure coming our way. Just the figure. Nothing else. It had to be Bray, I didn't know anyone else with that stride.

"Why is Bray here?" I asked aloud.

"What? Where?" Hunter said, looking around.

"Hey!" Bray shouted from a distance.

"How did you possibly know that was Bray?" Hunter asked, looking at me with wonder. "I couldn't even see him. He was, like, way over there, behind a tree—" His voice trailed off into thought.

"What happened? Sis? You okay?" Bray asked, his voice tainted with concern. "What did you have her doing? Are you hurt?"

"Slow down, she's not hurt—" Hunter paused. "You're not hurt, are you?"

"No," I shook my head. It felt like a heavy balloon.

"She was good, better than good. I was teaching her how to use her wings, and then, she caught on, and we raced, and well, she's super fast. But after she just collapsed. And then you came. And now, well, I don't have to tell you what's happening now," Hunter nervously explained.

"Well, I'm sure you're just worn out from a big day, sis. Let's get you to your feet." Bray grunted as he helped Hunter and me up.

We made our way slowly back down the path home. Maybe I was just exhausted from a long day. My hunger had since gone away, and all I could think about was sleeping.

———

I woke up on the couch in our quaint living room area. I could hear Mom and Dad whispering in the kitchen. I rubbed my groggy eyes and sat up, catching a couple of words from their conversation.

" —meeting tomorrow night," Dad whispered.

"But you only just got back. Do you have to go?" Mom asked with disappointment staining her voice. "Why can't the others go?"

"I know, Ina. It's just a meeting. It doesn't mean I'm going to be gone long. It's at Velrox, just the town to the north of us, so I will go and be back late tomorrow night." Dad comforted. "It's important that I attend these to keep informed as I travel."

Something caught my attention from the corner of my eye. Bray crept up and joined me on the emerald fabric couch. He pressed a finger to his lips and motioned to the kitchen. He must have been listening, too.

"Zandar—" Mom started.

"I'm going." Dad cut in. "They wouldn't ask so many of us to go if there wasn't a good reason. They won't be sending me to trade goods again for a little while. They stick to our regular rotations as always, you know that."

"Alright," Mom agreed. Not that she had much choice to or not. Dad didn't seem to be asking, just informing her.

"I'm going to bring Bray along this time," Dad noted.

I glanced at Bray. His eyes widened. The shadows made it hard to tell if he was excited or confuse, though I don't think he really knew what to feel. I don't think he had ever been to a meeting. And I don't think he had ever shown any interest in going to one before either.

"He's old enough to come along, and I think it would be good for him to come to this one being that it's just a day trip." Dad continued. "Why don't you and Esmari do something together, while us men are away?"

"That would be nice, it's been a while since we had some proper girl time," Mom said, her voice softer and less agitated than before.

"I know! Why don't you take her for her first trip to Sky Athra? Go get yourselves something nice," Dad soothed. His hands caressed her shoulders as he spoke. The iridescent yellow-green undertone of dad's wings caught the light for a moment, just like it usually did when he got an idea, before returning to the pale gray color. I see that color come out most on his wings when he is around mom.

Bray shifted beside me. He seemed perplexed as to why dad had the sudden interest in him coming along. Dad was so insistent in going, as well. *Was there something his conscience was telling him about this meeting?* Bray looked at me as if reading my mind. He nodded, probably thinking the same. Even still, I couldn't help but have excitement growing in my chest about finally visiting Sky Athra.

four

It was late morning when Bray and Dad joined some of the other men and headed for Velrox. Mom and I packed them lunches to have along the way and saw them off. Dad seemed chipper to tell Bray that morning about the trip, and while Bray happily accepted the invitation, I could tell he was still a bit skeptical. He seemed to fool Dad with his inquiries about the trip, as if we didn't listen in last night about it. And it wasn't long after they left that mom told me about our plans for the day.

"Dad thought it would be a fun idea for you and me to have a much-needed girl's day. What do you say that we head up to Sky Athra after we have some lunch? I can show you around and do a little shopping, and then we can pick a nice place to eat dinner tonight." Mom offered, her eyes twinkling with excitement.

"That sounds like fun!" I agreed, trying to show enough surprise.

"Wonderful! I'll help you get all dolled up, too. We will make a whole occasion out of it!" Mom cheered as she clasped my cheeks gently in her soft hands. She kissed my forehead before heading towards the kitchen. "I'll start on some lunch!"

The excitement grew once again in my chest for the exploration of Sky Athra. I had enjoyed seeing the wonderful lights from the ground all my life. And now I was finally going to experience the place for the first time. It was supposed to be sophisticated and classy, from what my classmates all said at least. Mom always would go to restaurants there for her lunch dates with friends and said the environment was like no other. She would tell me of the shopping they would do, and always would tell me how one day we would go there together. And to think that today was that day!

I joined mom in the kitchen. We prepared our

bacon, lettuce, tomato, and avocado sandwiches together at the countertop, and mom cut up some fresh fruits to have alongside. I poured us each a glass of iced tea before she and I sat at the table to eat. I took a great big bite of my sandwich and was caught off guard by the bursting flavors in my mouth. I could taste each ingredient so vividly. *I'm not sure if I will ever get used to how intense everything tastes now, but I wonder if the intensity wears off after a while or it just becomes the new normal.* I glanced at Mom, who was taking a drink of tea. She seemed unfazed by the flavors, so either she got used to it, or maybe she doesn't taste as vividly as I do. *Maybe she never did.* That was an odd thought to think about. I shook my head and smiled to myself.

"What's the matter, sweetie?" Mom asked, looking me over.

"Oh, nothing, just really good food," I responded quickly.

"Alright, well, eat up quickly, the sooner we are done, the sooner we can get ready!" Mom rang.

I think mom is just as excited about this as I am. Before long, we were getting ready to go. Mom put on some music as we got ready, just as she always did. She said that music helps you feel good about yourself when you get ready. Mom danced her way over to my closet to find some clothes for me.

"Now, what should you wear?" she mumbled

to herself. I heard her rustling through the hangers behind me as I sat by the mirror and started to do some makeup.

I heard her step back. The fabric brushed against her arm. I placed a hand on the ground and leaned back to check my makeup. I smiled for a moment, then my surroundings disappeared. *Navy blue loose-fit tank, gray skinny jeans, white button-down blouse with a small dirt smudge on the sleeve.*

"Which shirt do you want to wear?" Mom's voice broke through, and I was aware of my surroundings again.

"The blue seems right. The white has dirt on the sleeve," I said before I really could think.

"How— you didn't even turn around—" Mom stammered. "How did you know what color shirt I picked out for you?"

I turned to look at her. She seemed confused. *Was that true? Did I really not turn to look at them? But I saw them —*

"Huh, you're right. This one is dirty," Mom said, tossing it in my laundry basket and placing the other pieces of clothing on the bed. She seemed to move on. "Well, I like the blue one better too. Now, how about a high ponytail for your hair? It will keep it out of your way. I like your hair up."

Mom knelt behind me on the ground and styled my hair as I finished my makeup. When she was done, I got dressed and found a pair of earrings to match. Mom went off to get dressed and returned to my room just as I was slipping into some shoes. She used my mirror to put some lip tint on and came over to share some with me. We admired ourselves in the mirror for a moment.

"I think we look great!" Mom praised. I had to agree. I hadn't dressed like this, well, almost ever. I felt empowered. My wings seemed a little less out of place, too. "Let's get going."

We made our way down the path toward the center of town. I could see Sky Athra growing closer and closer. My heart pounded with excitement. Mom led us into "Things for Wings" where we were greeted by the owner.

"Welcome! Oh, Ina! It's nice to see you!" she said, her eyes twinkling with happiness at the sight of her old friend.

"Hello, Addie!" Mom smiled.

"What brings you in today?" Addie inquired, brushing the bangs of her black pixie cut out of her eyes with a pale-skinned hand. A few strands of white hair glimmered near her roots.

"We are heading to Sky Athra today. It's Esmari's first time," Mom noted.

"Ah! I heard that you had gotten your wings! Well, don't just stand there. I want to see them! Show those beauties off!" she cheered. Her face lighting up and her white swan-like wings flittering with excitement.

I backed up and slowly unfolded my wings, careful not to bump any of Addie's displays. My heart pounded, and I held my breath, searching her face for her reactions. She came over and gently examined my wings with her fingertips. Her eyes glittered as she analyzed them. My mom smiled softly at her friend.

"Well, would you look at that! They are very — unique." She chuckled. I tucked them back behind me, a bit embarrassed. They certainly weren't what she was expecting. "Esmari, our wings are like night and day! Dark and light!" Addie commented, lightening the mood a bit.

"Yeah, I suppose they are." I smiled back.

"I think they are simply divine!" Addie said, throwing up her arms with excitement. "Oh, and I have just the thing to celebrate the new you!" She danced off to the other side of the store.

"Addie, you really don't need to," Mom said lovingly.

"No, no! I insist. It's around here — somewhere — ah! Here it is. I made this recently after a dream I had. It's so different from what I usually make, but now I can see why the idea came to me! It matches your new look!" Addie expressed as she came with a small item in her hand. "Now, turn around so I can put it on you."

I glanced at mom, and she nodded for me to go along with it. Addie giggled with excitement as she clasped a necklace around my neck. It was light, and the metal chain was chilly against my warm collarbones. I reached down and felt a small uneven stone hanging from the chain. Addie led me gently to a mirror against the wall to see. Her hands rested on my shoulders, and her eyes sparkled with the light from the window. I examined the necklace. She was right, it did match. The stone was small and black with what seemed to be cracks like veins all throughout. I swayed from side to side in the light admiring how the stone had a fine sparkle throughout. It felt right, like it was always a part of me.

"Beautiful. It seems the necklace chose its owner this time," Addie whispered.

"How much do we owe you?" Mom asked as she too admired the necklace on me.

"Oh, nonsense! It's a gift! I couldn't imagine having you pay for a necklace that was so obviously meant for her owner! There's no one else in town that that could have worn this," Addie shooed. "Okay, I won't keep you any longer. Off you go on your adventure! You know the way!"

"Thank you," I said as we made our way to the open door at the back of her shop.

Mom hugged her friend goodbye and led us out of the doorway. There was a small pathway with shrubs on either side. The warm breeze played with my hair as I watched a couple take off toward Sky in front of us. They were hand in hand and flew so smoothly that they almost looked like they were floating into the unknown. Mom put an arm around me, and I grinned widely at her. She shook her head and laughed softly. She gently gave my shoulders an approving squeeze.

"Ready?" she asked. I nodded with excitement. "Alright. Just take your time, there's no rush. I will be right by your side. See the red arches? We will be flying to those; they indicate a safe spot to land."

I tried to calm my breathing. This was my mom's first time seeing me fly, and I didn't want to disappoint. Opening my wings carefully, I stepped away from Mom. She opened hers and fluttered up. I focused on my wings, silently checking their allegiance to me before liftoff. Then up I went. Mom's eyes glinted with soft tears of joy as I joined her. She took a quick breath, lowered her shoulders, and raised her chin with elegance as she led us up to Sky Athra.

The stone ground met my feet, and I gently tucked my wings away. My ears were met by music coming from speakers all through the walkways. The buildings were so sophisticated and modern. I could see lights from the theater flashing above some of the shops off in the distance. There was a bustle about the place. People everywhere I looked, going in and out of shops and chatting with friends. A sign to our left said, "Shopping Zone Ahead."

"Well, here we are!" Mom announced. "Be careful, it's usually pretty busy, so don't get lost. Try to stay close by, okay, dear?"

"It's so big!" I exclaimed.

"Let's go." Mom smiled. "There's a special place I want to start."

She led us down the walkway past stores of every kind. Some had accessories or shoes. Some had clothes. There was one store that was so simple inside with white walls and white floors, and only a couple of elegant dresses on display. The attendant of the store looked very uptight and professional. We passed a cafe with a very long line, but smelled delicious. Finally, we came up to a very tiny shop with lots of dark woods and red decor. Mom opened the door for me to enter.

"This is my favorite little spot to go before shopping. Pick whatever you would like." Mom said as we went up to the counter. On the wall was a simple menu of different flavors of smoothies listed.

"I'll just get whatever you are having," I

decided.

"Okay," Mom nodded then turned to ring a small golden bell on the counter. A short, older man came out from the back, wiping his hands on a towel. His eyes were kind and welcoming.

"Ahhhh," he sighed. "I haven't seen you in quite some time. And who's this? Must be your daughter."

"You know I had to bring her to the best place to get a delicious smoothie!" Mom boasted. The man gave out a hearty chuckle.

"Oh, you are too kind, too kind." He shook his head. "Alright, what will it be today."

"Blueberry banana. Two of them," Mom said.

We received our smoothies and left the store. Mom and I began our shopping endeavor while sipping on the delicious smoothies. It felt like a dream to finally be here. We entered a couple of clothing stores, and mom tried on some summer dresses. We enjoyed trying on several silly hats at another store, and laughing at each other in them. Mom picked out a new shirt for dad. It was late afternoon by the time we found a bench to take a break and relax for a bit.

"Having fun?" Mom asked as she finished off her smoothie and tossed it into the trash bin nearby. She sat back down beside me and patted my knee softly.

"Yes, I forgot how exhausting shopping was, though!" I groaned dramatically.

"You haven't found anything you like yet?" Mom asked with a little bit of disappointment tainting her voice.

"Not yet. Nothing has really jumped out at me," I remarked.

"Okay," Mom sighed.

"But I think I might just be distracted by the scenery! I'm sure I'll find something soon." I quickly added, flashing her a big smile. Truth was, everything I was trying was something I usually wore, but, for some reason, just didn't feel right on me anymore. I wanted something new, something I felt confident in.

"Then, off we go! We will find you just what you need," Mom stated proudly. It was nice to see the lighter side of her. Less formal.

We looked around at a few more shops. I agreed to get a pair of shorts that Mom really liked on me, which made her happy. A shop or two later, I picked out a shirt to go with them. As the sun began to go down, the colorful lights on the shops came on, creating an entirely new environment to be in. There was a glow to the pavement as well, which was mesmerizing to watch as we walked. Mom wanted to find both of us some new shoes to go with the clothes we picked up. We found a nice-looking shoe store with lots of variety.

Inside, there was a friendly attendant who pointed us in the right direction for our sizes. I helped mom pick out some shoes to go along with her dress; sandals with tan straps across the top. The attendant informed us that they were having a sale on the sandals and set the shoes aside up front for us to keep looking. I found myself gravitating to some sandals as well, and decided to try them on. Mom and I chatted about color options of the sandals, debating what would work best for my new outfit. Another customer entered the store and began discussing something with the attendant.

"I like how these fit," I told Mom as I knelt on the ground to take them off. Something banged on the cashier's counter and echoed in the store, making Mom and me both jump. I lost my balance for a moment, slamming my hand into the carpeted floor to catch myself.

Suddenly, my surroundings disappeared. *Tall male, rough appearance, small scar on jawline, well dressed. He's agitated. He's turning his head, looking at me —*

I gasped. My surroundings came back to me. His black eyes were so harsh. I looked around; I couldn't see him from where I was. How was that possible? I just saw him so clearly, and he looked right at me. I heard the customer abruptly leave the store, slamming against the door as he left. Mom and I exchanged looks. She shrugged at me, not seeming to notice that anything happened with me. The attendant came over to us with a customer service smile pasted on his face.

"How is everything going over here? Find anything you are interested in, Miss?" He said to me, ignoring what had just happened with the other customer.

"I'll take these," I said, handing them to him as I put my shoes back on. "Was everything okay with that other customer?"

"Um—yes, yes. All fine." He nervously laughed, "He was just someone from another town looking for something I couldn't help him with."

The attendant rang up our items, and mom paid. We thanked the man and left to find a restaurant to eat at for dinner.

I picked a cafe that had outdoor seating, so we could people watch while we ate. In the distance, we could hear the bass of some music begin to play at a dance club. Before long, our server brought our food to our table. Mom and I shared a sandwich and a salad while she chatted away. I wasn't paying much attention to her, though. My mind was still caught up on the man from the shoe store. His piercing eyes flashed in my head again. It felt like he was staring right through me. The feeling sent a chill down my spine. Something wasn't right about it.

five

I slept in late the next day, finding myself exhausted from the shopping trip the day before. When I finally got up, it was late morning and already warm in my room from the sun shining in my window. I changed into my new outfit, admiring my new necklace once again. Something about the necklace felt soothing to have on. I made my way to the kitchen, where I found Mom had baked a fresh batch of banana nut muffins and left them on the counter to cool. Taking one, I sat at the table and took a big bite. *Still warm.*

"Mornin' sis," Bray said, tugging gently on my ponytail. I jumped.

"Didn't know anyone was home. It was so quiet," I remarked.

"Mom and Dad went out already," Bray said, grabbing a muffin, too. He plopped down in the chair across from me and shoved the entire muffin in his mouth.

"Nice," I said sarcastically. "How was the meeting yesterday?"

"Oh, that's right, we got back so late that you were already asleep," he mumbled through a mouth full of muffin. I eyed him with disgust. Quickly, he chewed and swallowed, before continuing. "It was not all that exciting for the most of it, just business stuff. But they were talking about how there was word of an increase of visitors from other towns. They said that someone thought a Royal was traveling through, but there were also travelers that were causing some trouble. Particularly, a man and some people who seemed to be with him. So, they were informing everyone to be cautious. It's possible that a Royal would be coming through our town, though. The guy said that, while they didn't know for sure, they seemed to be looking for someone or something."

"Huh, that's interesting. We haven't had a Royal here in a while. I wonder if we will do a festival. I remember when I was really little we had some sort of festival when there was a Royal here," I thought out loud.

"Yeah, I don't know. Probably. I was little, too, when we had the last one, but I remember there were games and competitions and stuff," Bray explained. "With an event like this, though, I can't imagine that they wouldn't do another festival. Okay, I'm off."

"Where are you headed?" I asked. "You got a date?"

"Yeah, I'm gonna go win over a girl's heart!" he teased, holding his hands to his chest with a dreamy expression on his face.

"Good luck with that," I laughed.

"You have no confidence in me, sis." Bray frowned.

"And you have muffin stuck to your face," I noted.

Bray frantically wiped at his face, and I just shook my head. As Bray was leaving out the back door, Hunter came crashing through with excitement all over his face. He had so much energy, he nearly pushed Bray over to get through. The commotion was such a funny sight, I found myself laughing right out loud.

"Guess what!" he shouted, grabbing Bray by the shoulders. Bray raised his eyebrows at him and flexed a little, to intimidate him. He raised his wings out and stared Hunter in the face. I shook my head at his ridiculous display of masculinity. Hunter's eyes widened. He released his hands and smoothed Bray's shirt nervously.

"What's the big news, Hunter?' I said.

"Oh—um—" Hunter started trying to find his thought again. He turned to me, and the excitement returned to his face. "The town's having a festival tonight. I guess there's word that a Royal is in town. The businesses were just informed that so they could close down early for the festivities." Hunter was nearly jumping up and down from the excitement.

"Well, I guess that answer's our question," Bray noted, before shutting the door behind him.

"Isn't this just so awesome! I mean, to think, we might actually meet a Royal! I wonder what they will look like. Will they be dressed in some sort of ancient attire?" Hunter rambled on. "Maybe they will use their powers to do some magic or something."

"I don't think that's how that works." I chuckled as Hunter slumped into the chair next to me, deep in thought. He didn't seem to hear me.

"How will we know who they are? It could be anyone! I wonder why they are even here?" Hunter continued. Suddenly, he looked at me. Leaning in real close, he whispered, "maybe they are here to take someone away to their secret hideaway with them."

"You're such a goofball," I replied, pushing him away.

"You never know!" Hunter defended.

My mind went to Ruby. *She loves the festivals we have. I wonder if she heard yet.*

"Aaaand she's gone," Hunter said, staring me down. "Where do you go when you zone out like that?"

"I was just thinking of Ruby, want to come with me to tell her about the festival?" I asked.

"Sure," Hunter shrugged.

I cleaned up my muffin wrapper and crumbs, and we headed out across town to Ruby's. The warmth of the sun wrapped around us as we walked. A breeze danced through a nearby bush and kicked up some red dust by our feet. We made our way past the shops, many of which were already putting up fancy decor for the afternoon. Hunter chatted away with excitement about the Royal, and I listened. He was like a kid trying candy for the first time. Before long, we arrived at Ruby's home.

"Well, well, well!" Ruby greeted, standing up from the ground. She brushed her muddy hands on a checkered gardening apron. "Come inside! Let me wash up. Where are we headed today?"

"Hmmm—" I thought, "The woods."

Hunter and I followed Ruby into her home, which was considerably cleaner than the last time I was over. The bookshelves were all back in order, and you could again see the entire floor. Hunter was still looking at me, a bit confused about our destination, but soon enough, Ruby was bringing out the tea, and I didn't bother explaining to him.

"Well? I told you, didn't I?" Ruby said, motioning to my wings as she placed the tray on the coffee table. "Let's see them!"

I had forgotten that she hadn't seen my wings yet, and suddenly became almost as excited to show her as Hunter was about the festival. I presented the wings, and Ruby motioned for me to turn for her. I happily obliged, twirling a few times so she could see them from every angle. She clasped her hands together and giggled with glee.

"What do you think?" I asked, fully aware of her answer based on the pride in her eyes.

"Wonderful," she stated with a satisfied nod. I joined her and Hunter, and took a small slurp of the warm tea. "Now, Miss Esmari, I know that's not the only reason you came by today. Although, I thoroughly enjoyed seeing your newest addition."

Hunter looked giddily at me, barely able to sit still. I rolled my eyes at him. "Go on," I said.

"A Royal has come to *our* town!" He exclaimed. "And there's going to be a whole festival for it and everything! With food, and games, and music! My parents got word this morning so that they could close down the shop early for it."

"Well, isn't that something!" Ruby gasped.

"They haven't unveiled their motives yet, however, but I have my theories," Hunter pondered.

"Will you come?" I asked Ruby eagerly.

"Oh, well, of course! And I just got my new outfit from your parents' shop, Hunter. What a perfect way to break it in," Ruby noted. "I'm with Hunter on this, I wonder why they are here too. I want to know your theories."

I shook my head and chuckled. *Oh, now she's done it for sure.* Hunter's eyes lit up even brighter than before. Before we knew it, Hunter was rambling on about his theories of the Royal, each idea more extravagant than the last.

———

It was late afternoon by the time Hunter, Ruby, and I made our way to the festival. There was such a bustle throughout the area. Kids were laughing and playing games together as their parents watched and applauded for them. Papers were hung around, explaining where to find different activities that were going to be held. Mom and Dad waved at us from over by a shop as they chatted with a group of their friends. We stopped by a table handing out free shaved ice to enjoy. I decided on grape flavoring.

"Hey, sis!" Bray called from behind; he and one of his friends parted ways as he came over to us. We retrieved our snow cones and stepped aside.

"Hi, Bray," I nodded, digging my plastic spoon into my shaved ice and carving off a worthy bite.

"There's a wing race over behind the ice cream shop. My friends and I signed up, you gonna come cheer your handsome older brother on?" Bray persuaded.

"No, but I'll be there to watch you get beat," I sassed.

Bray ticked his tongue and snagged my and Hunter's arms, sending my perfect icy bite flopping to the ground. "Come on, it'll be fun."

I frowned and waved a quick goodbye with my plastic spoon at Ruby, who was chuckling at the encounter through a mouthful of her shaved ice. We were involuntarily dragged to the race field, where there were some spectator chairs set up. Hunter and I found some a couple of seats together toward the back. Bray joined his friends and competitors at the start line, shaking their hands and joking with one another.

"You're pretty fast, too. Maybe you should sign up for the next race?" Hunter smirked.

"Not interested," I lied. It actually did sound fun, but I'm not all that fast, nor experienced enough. Plus, racing was kind of Bray's thing. I didn't want to take that over. I shoved a large bite of syrupy ice into my mouth and glanced over to see Mom and Dad joining the small crowd with their friends. A woman and man sat in front of us in the two vacant chairs.

"Racers, please make your way to the starting line!" called a raspy-voiced man through a megaphone. A few more racers joined Bray and the others at the start line. They all began to hover above the ground. "Everyone know the rules? There and back, no rough play. At the sound of my whistle!"

The racers became focused, spacing out to allow for enough flying room. The man blew the whistle, and the racers dashed off. The crowd cheered loudly; Hunter screamed beside me and waved his hands in the air. The racers built up speed and flew off in the distance. Everyone continued to cheer on their racers, waiting eagerly to see who would return to the line first. The woman in front of me shifted in her seat, but remained quiet. The golden beads and charms in her long black braids chimed together. The racers came back into view, sweat glistening on their faces. Bray and another man were neck and neck for first place, with several other racers close behind. They grew closer and closer to the finish line. The crowd stood to their feet with excitement, cheering as loudly as they could as they crossed the line. Hunter and I jumped up and down, cheering Bray's name.

"What a close race! First place goes to Stanley, with Bray in a close second and followed by Gunner in third!" announced the raspy-voiced man. "Winners, please come find me for your prizes! Our next race will start in a half-hour. Enjoy the festival, everyone!"

"Let's go congratulate him," Hunter said as he collected my now empty cup and tossed it in a trash bin just behind us.

"Hold on, we need to wait till the crowd dies out a little. He's getting his prize right now anyway," I stated.

The woman in front of me leaned to the man

next to her and spoke something into his ear. She seemed uninterested in the results of the race. The two of them stood together and began to make their way elsewhere. *Why watch if you aren't interested? Maybe the man wanted to come.* The woman turned slightly to avoid a little girl running past. Her elegant wings flittered slightly. They looked like dripping pewter and glistened with a subtle golden tone that matched the undertones of her beautiful chocolate skin. But something else shone on her wing. She smiled softly at the little girl and turned back. For a split second, I caught a glimpse of a small metallic copper smear on the bottom of her left wing, just as she tucked her wings back away and continued on her way. *Were my eyes playing tricks on me?* Before I could think, I pushed past Hunter.

"Hey! Where are you going?" Hunter called to me.

I didn't have time to answer. I needed to find her. I needed to know if what I saw was real. Why did she have the same smear on her wing? Maybe we were supposed to be connected somehow? I felt this urge to know, like nothing else mattered. Something deep inside me was telling me that she was important to me. I weaved and bobbed my way through the crowd, my heart pounding. Finally getting close enough to call out to her.

"Wait!" I called. But she didn't hear me.

I ran past person after person, pushing my way through. I'd lose her for a moment, and then, a second later, spot her braids or the shimmer of her wings. She didn't look like she was rushing, but I was having the worst luck pushing through the crowd. Someone bumped into me, making me fall to the ground. I sat for a moment, collecting my bearings. I pushed my hands against the dirt to help me get up. My surroundings faded for a moment, just as they had before, and I saw her figure clear in my head. Something was in her hand. *What is that? Shaved ice!* My surroundings came back to me. *How did I just do that?* I shook my head. I couldn't focus on that right now. I needed to find her. *She's by the shaved ice table.* I ran to find that table. She was turning to leave, I reached out and grabbed her arm.

"Wait!" I pleaded, catching my breath.

Her arm tensed and then softened at the surprise of my touch. I released her arm. She turned to look at me. Her face was serious but beautiful and dignified. She looked me over with eyes of grays and browns. They reminded me of pine tree bark. I was taken aback by her presence.

"I'm sorry, but your wings—" I started. I didn't really think about what I was going to say if I really did catch up to her. Her eyes widened slightly, observing me a bit more intensely.

"Yes?" she finally said, her voice had a smooth quality that reminded me of honey. But something about the slight accent in that single word she spoke made me feel out of place in the presence of her exotic beauty.

"Back at the race, I caught a glimpse of something on your wing, but I didn't see it very clearly. I had to know if I was just seeing things. If it was like mine," I rambled, still out of breath from the chase.

"Like yours?" she whispered, eyeing the man at her side.

"I mean— I only saw it for a moment—" I stuttered. I looked down. *Just spit it out, Esmari.* I took a deep breath. "Do you have a copper smear on your wing?"

Her face didn't change the observant expression, but she turned her head to face me dead on. Her shoulders lowered, ever so slightly. I must have taken her completely off guard. I could see in her eyes that she was processing and thinking. *Maybe this was a bad idea. Maybe she's just as unhappy about the copper on her wing as I am with it on mine.* A guilty feeling rose up in my gut. She looked me over again.

"Come with me," she said in a way I didn't question. She led us to a less crowded area behind some shops. A few mothers were sitting with their young children under a shady tree just out of earshot.

"I'm sorry—" I muttered. I couldn't read her. I didn't know if she was angry with me. I didn't know what to say.

"Which wing?" she asked. *Was she quizzing me now?*

"On your left wing. Just like mine," I said hesitantly.

She paused. "Show me."

I opened my wings carefully. I was shaking with terror, or anxiety, not really sure which. My heart pounded. Slowly, I turned for her to see. We stood in silence for quite some time. *Why isn't she saying anything?* Finally, she sighed sharply. I tucked my wings back and turned to look at her and the man who still stood with us. She stood tall with her chin high. Her eyes softened, and she smiled gently.

She turned to the man. "Send word to Agathin, that we will be heading home tomorrow."

The man nodded and turned to fly off. For a moment, he paused and flashed me a smile, then off he went. The woman turned back to me and looked me over again. I felt very self-conscious and tugged at my shirt to pull it down. Even though she was now seemingly pleased, her face was still stern and serious. It was as if she was analyzing me.

"Interesting that you found us. I'm usually pretty good at noticing. But you, you are different for me. Though it has been a while," she whispered to herself. I felt lost and confused. "You were sitting behind me at the race, were you not?"

"Yes," I answered.

"Ah, that explains the feeling," the woman said. "What is your name?"

"Esmari," I stated.

"Hello, Esmari. I am Maya," introduced the woman. She shook my hand with strength and certainty. I, on the other hand, felt awkward and out of place. She dropped my hand and turned away from me as if she was taking into consideration of what to say. "Do you know why Athra is having a festival today?"

I paused. What an odd question. Everyone knew why, didn't they? "There's a Royal here," I said carefully. Maya turned to me and raised an eyebrow. It clicked. "You're the Royal, aren't you?"

Maya nodded with a smirk on her face. I took a sharp breath in. *I'm in the presence of Royalty. What should I say? Do I bow? Is that a thing? I don't know how to act around a Royal.* A wave of embarrassment crashed through my chest. *I just grabbed a Royal's arm. I didn't know she was a Royal when I did that!*

Was she angry with me?

"Do you know why I am here?" Maya asked. I snapped out of my thoughts and took in her question for a moment.

I shook my head. *How was I supposed to know?*

"Because of you."

"Me? Why would you be here because of me?" I chuckled uncomfortably.

"Let me ask you something else. What do you know about Royals?" Maya asked.

"Not much," I stated. She stayed quiet, waiting for my answer. "Okay, well, they're secretive. Royals are women. They have some kind of power. They keep the peace. They are chosen—"

"Chosen how?" Maya chimed.

Why doesn't she just explain it to me? "I don't know," I shrugged, trying to keep the slight agitation out of my voice. "Some defining factor, only they know about."

"Not just a factor. A mark," she stated matter-of-factly. "Was there anything when you got your wings that was odd? Something you saw, but others seemed to not notice?"

"Uh—I— got my wings late," I stuttered. The question caught me off guard. I thought for a moment. *There was a lot that was odd when I got my wings. They didn't seem to suit me. And then there's the whole flavors-being-more-intense thing. The cracks on my wings were odd, not to mention —* "Wait. The copper smear? Hunter shrugged it off as if he didn't even see it."

Maya stared at me for a moment then looked down at the ground. Her face was calm, with a slight smirk on her lips again. She breathed out a silent chuckle through her nose before looking back up at me. It was as if she didn't want to explain; she wanted me to come to the conclusions on my own. It was a bit irritating. *Why was she asking me so many questions? What was she looking for me to understand?* My gut dropped. *That's it isn't it? That's the mark.*

"You can't be serious," I said in disbelief. Maya only tilted her head and smiled with a raise of her eyebrow. "You're serious, aren't you? The copper? That's the mark of Royalty? That means—" My heart pounded in my chest.

"Yep," Maya said with satisfaction and a tinge of arrogance.

"I'm a Royal?"

six

I stood in disbelief. I felt like someone knocked the wind out of me. I couldn't breathe. I couldn't think. I felt like the entire world was moving without me. It had to be some cruel joke. There was no way this was real. *Why me?* Maya continued to watch me. I was waiting for her to say something, but she never did. She just watched as everything I knew about myself came to a crashing halt

"There you are!" Hunter called. "I've been

looking everywhere for you! You just ran off without a word and — "

I looked at him, still processing everything. "Sorry," I muttered.

"Who's she?" Hunter whispered into my ear. "Are you okay? Did she do something to hurt you?"

"No, no," I shook my head hurriedly. Hunter frowned, looking very confused. I looked at Maya, then at Hunter. *What was I supposed to say?*

"I'm Maya," she greeted.

"Hunter," he said quizzically.

"Esmari was just about to invite me to dinner to meet her family. You must be a friend of hers, will you be joining us?" Maya diverted, sounding friendly.

"Uh— yeah—" I stammered, finding my voice again. "Hunter's a good friend of mine."

"Do you think we could meet at your house and we can discuss things further? You can collect your family, and I'm sure Hunter won't mind showing me the way," Maya suggested definitively. I nodded, not really feeling like I had much of a choice.

Hunter looked at me for guidance. The whole conversation felt odd to the both of us. I waved him on, and he left with Maya towards my home while I set off to find my parents and brother. I thankfully found them together, not far from where I was, enjoying some of the festival treats.

"Hey, sis! Did you see the race?" Bray boasted with glee.

"Uh, yeah," I said. "I saw you lose."

"Ha!" Dad laughed.

"So," I started. *How was I supposed to tell them about all of what just happened? Maya was already on her way to the house.*

"What is it, Esmari? You seem like something has happened." Mom cooed in a hushed tone.

I glanced around. There weren't many people around to hear us. "I, um," *Just spit it out, Esmari!* "I met a Royal. And she's —well— she's invited herself over for dinner this evening." The words didn't even sound believable.

"Ha! Come on, sis, what's up?" Bray laughed, nudging me. I looked at him and then at Mom and Dad.

"I don't think she's kidding," Dad said, his voice stained with awe. I shook my head, Bray's eyes widened as it sank in.

"Oh!" Mom gasped. "When?"

I gritted my teeth. "Hunter is taking her there right now."

"Oh, well, we really shouldn't keep them waiting!" Mom said flustered, grabbing my arm and starting to the house. "What should I make?

Our house is really not suited well for a Royal! I hope that it's clean enough. Good thing I picked up some this morning!"

Dad patted her arm. "Ina, I'm sure it's fine."

"We are going to meet a Royal! This is quite a day. To think that I'm going to serve a Royal at our home!" Mom rambled anxiously.

"Yeah," I sighed. *Two actually.* I swallowed hard and looked at the ground watching the familiar red dust puff around our feet. With every step we took closer to the house, I grew more and more uneasy.

"You think she saw my race?" Bray asked.

"Yeah, she was there," I said.

"Ah, no way!" Bray exclaimed.

We approached the house, and I could see Hunter, Maya, and the man from before, all waiting alongside the back door. Hunter and the man were chatting, and Maya was listening calmly. Mom smoothed her dress and fixed her hair nervously. She turned to me and fixed my hair, too. I could feel her excitement through her hands as she fussed. Bray straightened his posture as if to make himself more dignified and presentable. Hunter caught my attention and waved excitedly as if we hadn't just seen each other.

"Hello, you must be Esmari's family," Maya said with grace. She shook Mom's hand gently then

Dad's. "I'm Maya, and this is Corbin. Please forgive us for the short notice."

"Hello. I'm Zander, and this is my wife, Ina, and our son, Bray. Please, come in!" Dad greeted pridefully. He opened the door for everyone to enter. Hunter snuck to my side.

"Thank goodness you came when you did! I was running out of stories to entertain them with!" Hunter whispered in my ear as we followed the others into the house. I smirked at him. His silly presence put me more at ease.

By the time we entered, mom was already working away at making some chicken and rice for our dinner. The aroma of a multitude of seasonings filled the air. Dad had invited Maya and Corbin to the living room. Hunter, Bray, and I prepared some glasses of iced tea for everyone and brought it to them. Bray and Dad chatted with Maya about the festival and the race as well as the recent events brought up in the meeting they had attended. My mind lingered over the different notes of flavors in the tea dripping down my throat. Before long, Mom invited everyone to the dinner table to eat. Maya stepped close to me, stopping me in the living room.

"You didn't tell them," she said. It wasn't a question. I shook my head and looked at my feet, unsure of what to say. I felt like a small child in the presence of her Royalty. For a moment, I was shrinking smaller and smaller as more of my confidence disappeared. She laid a soft hand on my shoulder, and I glanced up at her smiling face. It was as if she understood that I was still processing everything. She nodded to the kitchen and walked beside me to find a seat.

"I'm sorry, it's not much." Mom fussed.

"Thank you, I appreciate the home-cooked meal," Maya said, taking a seat next to Corbin. We all began to eat in a silence tainted with anticipation. Maya took a bite and looked as if she was carefully considering her next words.

Corbin looked at me and smiled. His cleanly trimmed beard and mustache suited his kind pale face. He had a warmth about him. He took another bite of the food and adjusted the ponytail of his long wavy black hair. He nodded at me subtly, then leaned and whispered into Maya's ear. She nodded back in satisfaction of his words. I felt awkward and out of place here. I wanted to run away and hide. Fear came over me. I took a breath and forced myself to eat. Mom's cooking couldn't even calm my nerves today.

"The food is very delicious, Ina," Corbin said, bringing conversation back into the room.

"Oh, well, thank you! There's plenty more, so please help yourself!" Mom beamed.

"I'd like to apologize again for imposing on you all this evening. But there is something that I need to discuss with all of you, if I may," Maya said gently.

"No need to apologize. There's always space at our table." Dad smiled back. "Please, what is it?"

Maya folded her hands in front of her and glanced at me from the corner of her eye. "Corbin and I will be heading back to our home tomorrow. And, hopefully, Esmari will agree to join us." Her gaze fell to Mom and Dad. I clenched my jaw. "Your daughter, Esmari, is a Royal."

Bray coughed and nearly spit his tea. His eyes widened and shot at me. I looked down. I could feel the tension and surprise thicken the air in the room. I looked at Hunter, who kept opening and closing his mouth, making no sound. Mom looked at Dad and caught his hand with hers, grasping for some sort of stability. Dad looked down at his plate, still processing the words Maya had said.

After a moment, Maya continued, "I realize this is quite a lot to take in. I was sent to find the new Royal and bring her to live with others like her. She would learn everything she needs to know. She is, of course, allowed to bring someone to accompany her, though we generally suggest not to bring anyone of blood relation."

"This is—" Dad started then paused. He

seemed to be searching for the right words to say. He looked at Mom as if hoping to find the words written on her face.

Mom's eyes caught mine. "Is this what you want to do? Do you want to go with them?" Her question was sincere. It caught me off guard. Up until that point, I didn't realize I had a choice to make. I felt uneasy, but something inside me was telling me I had to go.

"Yes. I think I want to go," I said. It was the easiest words I had spoken all afternoon. Maya looked at me with pride in her eyes.

"I am so glad," she exclaimed softly. "Now, in terms of accompanying. You don't have to bring anyone along, but you are welcome to."

I looked at Hunter hopeful. "Me?" he said, pointing at his chest in disbelief. I nodded and smiled. He grinned widely.

"It's settled then," Maya said with satisfaction. "We will leave tomorrow. You won't need to pack much; any clothes and necessities will be available to the both of you at your new home. But, if there is anything else you would like to have with you, I suggest you pack it up. You won't be coming back. You will, of course, be allowed to write to your family, and they can send letters back with the help of someone like Corbin. Please understand, though, that we cannot disclose where your new home will be, that includes telling your own family."

I looked around the table. It hit me, this time tomorrow, I will no longer be calling this place home. I won't be sitting down for dinner with my parents and brother again. I won't be watching my parents from across the table, chatting lovingly. I won't be playfully teased by my brother about how I'm eating my food. I simply won't be here. It all happened so fast. It didn't feel real. Mom looked at me with tears in her eyes. I think it occurred to her, too. Dad sat tall and proud. Bray sat staring at his now empty plate. He didn't say a word. I suddenly longed for him to tease me like he always did, for him to give me a hard time. He said nothing. Quietly he stood.

"Excuse me," he said and left the room, never looking up at anyone.

My gaze lingered on the now empty doorway for a moment. A feeling of longing crept up my throat as I sat, hoping Bray would rejoin us. But, something in me knew he wouldn't. I swallowed hard, dropping my head to stare back down at my plate.

"Corbin, why don't you join Hunter back to his place. His family will need to know. You can discuss what will be expected of him along the way," Maya suggested.

"Sure," Corbin said happily. "I look forward to

seeing the family you've talked about!"

Hunter stood excitedly. "Uh, great!" he said anxiously. "I'll come by tomorrow morning, Es. Thanks for dinner!" They waved goodbye and headed out the door as Mom began to collect the dishes from the table.

"Thank you, Ina. Everything was delicious," Maya said.

"Of course. I'm so happy you liked it." Mom beamed as she looked me over.

Dad relaxed back in his chair. He crossed his arms and smiled softly. "You're sure about this?" he asked me.

"I mean," I hesitated. "It's all a crazy idea. And it's all happened so fast. I feel like I just got my wings, and now this. But, something in my gut is telling me that I need to go."

Maya laid a hand on my shoulder and sighed. "I know. I'm sorry for the rushed nature of this. You are making the right choice. You are a Royal. You will be surrounded by others like you who can help you understand and achieve your full potential." Her reassuring voice put me at ease.

"If you are sure, then your mother and I will support your decision," Dad said. Mom put her hands on Dad's shoulders. I felt a growing sadness in my chest.

"I'm sure you have many questions, and I

promise to answer what I can, but just not tonight. I think it is time I took my leave. Tomorrow, I will come to collect you and Hunter, and we will head out together. Try to get some sleep tonight." Maya instructed. She stood from the table and thanked Mom and Dad for the hospitality, then left. Mom, Dad, and I sat in silence for a moment, lost for what to say to each other. I couldn't bear it anymore.

"So," I said, still searching for a direction for the sentence leaving my lips. "Wild day, huh?"

Mom laughed. "Who would have thought that we would have a Royal in our family?"

"Who would have thought the late bloomer daughter of yours would be the Royal?" I remarked.

"You're really leaving," Mom said with a lump in her throat. Tears welled up in her eyes.

"Mom," I pleaded. I didn't want her to cry. Seeing her cry made my heart sink. I thought for a moment. "Can you maybe help me pack?"

Mom wiped her tear-stained cheeks and pressed her lips together, taking a big breath. "Yes, sweetie. I can do that."

We headed to my room, and my mind was unfocused. It all felt so unreal. I'd never packed to go anywhere before. Mom found an old backpack of hers for me to use. It made me happy to see the navy-colored canvas bag in her hands and brought so many distant memories to the surface. I looked around my room at little trinkets and things I had gotten through the years. Nothing really jumped out at me as important to bring. Mom found a photo of our family and tucked it in an unused leather journal. She smiled and placed it in the bag for me. We chatted and imagined what my new home would look like. Mom seemed to be just as conflicted as I was on how to feel about all of this. Dad came in and tucked a folded paper in the book as well, telling me to open it when I got settled down and needed a reminder of home. Then, he ushered mom out of the room, advising me to get some sleep.

I got myself ready for bed, but was much too anxious to sleep. My mind was combing over different items in my room, trying to be sure there wasn't anything else I wanted to bring along. I imagined what the trip would be like tomorrow as I played with the necklace Addie gave me that remained on my neck. I thought about Ruby and how I wasn't even going to have a chance to say goodbye. *If I hadn't chased after Maya, if I hadn't seen the mark, would she have even noticed me? Would I be leaving everything and everyone I ever knew?* I shook my head. Going over to the mirror, I analyzed my wings again. *How could I be a Royal?* I stared at my reflection. *There isn't anything special about me. What if this was a mistake?*

My mind went to Bray. He hadn't said a word to me almost all night. I wanted to know what was going through his head. I opened my door and tiptoed into the hallway. The house was dark and quiet, but I could still see the sliver of light coming from under Bray's bedroom door. I snuck into the kitchen and carefully opened the cupboard, making as little sound as possible. I snagged the peanut butter and a bowl. Taking out two spoons from the drawer, I used one to place a massive glob of peanut butter in the bowl. I returned the peanut butter container to its spot in the cupboard and stuck both spoons in the bowl, before creeping my way down to Bray's room. With a single finger, I tapped my nail on his door, hoping not to wake my parents. To my relief, he opened his door. I raised my peanut butter offering, and he smiled at me. Entering his room, I closed the door behind me.

Bray and I sat on the floor, and each took a bite of peanut butter. It was something we had done since we were little. Mom would always mention that she didn't understand how our family went through the peanut butter so quickly, but Bray and I knew it was us. We never told her. It was our little secret, and we wanted to keep it that way.

"So," I broke the ice.

"So," Bray said, taking another lick of peanut

butter.

"You hardly said anything tonight," I stated, looking at the floor.

"What did you want me to say?" Bray asked.

"I don't know," I sighed. "Are you mad?"

Bray looked at me and took a deep breath. "No," he said. "I just don't know what to think of it. I guess part of me knew something was off when you got your wings. It was so different for you. It was scary different. But I guess I just didn't think that this was the reason."

"Yeah, if it helps any, it was just as much of a surprise to me," I told him. I licked more peanut butter off of my spoon.

"How did she find you?" Bray asked.

"Well, I kind of found her. After your race, she was leaving and after chasing after her and falling in the dirt—" I rambled.

"You literally fell head over heels for the Royal," Bray teased.

"No! It wasn't like that, some guy bumped into me, and I fell—" I tried to explain.

"Are you really going?" he asked, his expression suddenly turning serious again.

"I'm really going," I confirmed.

"Are you scared?"

"Yeah, I suppose so. A little bit. It's more anxious, though. Anxious to know, anxious to understand. I mean, everything we are ever taught about Royals is pure speculation and rumors, and I'm actually going to know what's true and what's not." I said. Bray placed his spoon in the now-empty bowl, and laid back on the floor, staring at the ceiling.

"What do you think it's going to be like?" he asked.

I tossed a pillow to him from his bed, and he tucked it under his head. I pondered on the question for a moment. "I don't know," I said finally.

"You think you have powers or whatever?" he said.

"I guess I might. But I don't know what they are." I shrugged.

"Do you feel different now that you've got your wings?" Bray asked.

"Yeah, sorta," I remarked. "Food tastes different. Like more flavorful somehow. Dad thought it was my imagination. But I noticed it the very first time I ate after I got my wings."

"Huh, I think you're just crazy," Bray smirked.

"Hey! You asked! Don't be calling your Royal sister crazy!" I gawked, smacking his leg.

"My apologies, your Royal-ness," he teased. I laughed and rolled my eyes at him. I realized just how much I was going to miss being here.

Everything is going to change.

"It's going to be weird. I've never even been out of Athra," I said.

"Yeah," Bray sighed.

"And I'm not going to know anyone there," I said, fear filling my gut.

"Are you having second thoughts?" Bray asked.

"Yeah. No. Maybe? I don't know." I sighed. "I'm having to drop everything. It's just a huge decision I made tonight."

"You can change your mind, you know," Bray said softly.

"I know. But I think I need to go." I said. He nodded with understanding.

"Okay, sis, you crashing in here or your room?" he asked.

"Mine, I suppose," I said, standing up slowly and shaking my half numb foot. "See you in the morning."

I took the bowl and spoons out to the kitchen and washed them before placing them in the drying rack with the other dishes. For a moment, I just stood there in the kitchen waiting, listening. I soaked in the silence of the home. That feeling of safety wrapped its comforting arms around me like a great big bear hug that I didn't want to dismiss. I could hear the subtle whooshing sound of the fan that always stayed on in the living room. The occasional hum that our fridge made, which always sounded so much louder in the night. I listened for the ticking of the wall clock that hung nearby, which still to this day ran slow. Tick, tock, tick, tock. I was going to miss all of this.

Quietly, I snuck back into my room and crawled into bed. Thinking back on my talk with Bray put my mind at ease. Through the dim moonlight, I took one last look around my bedroom before I closed my eyes, and I drifted off to sleep.

seven

It was late the next morning when I woke to the sound of Mom clanking in the kitchen. It was a familiar sound of her whisk tapping against a glass mixing bowl, which made me smile to myself. I jumped out of bed and dressed. Excited for the day, I made my way out to the kitchen, brushing my hair along the way. Mom was humming away as she baked. The fragrance of her blueberry muffins filled the air. I smiled as I watched Dad kiss her cheek and take a seat at the table with a mug of steaming coffee in hand. He caught a glimpse of me standing in the doorway and grinned.

"Good morning," he greeted. There was a knock on the door as it opened. I turned to see Hunter making his way into the house.

"Hey!" he waved. He was chipper as ever this morning as he hung his bag on a hook by the door.

"Good morning, Hunter. There are fresh muffins, straight out of the oven if you would like one," Mom called over her shoulder as she washed the batter off her hands.

"Ah! Would I ever!" Hunter exclaimed. He grabbed a hot blueberry muffin from the pan and bounced it from hand to hand before landing it on a napkin and setting it on the table. I laughed.

I grabbed a muffin and joined Dad and Hunter at the table. Mom poured us each a small glass of orange juice. I could hear Bray's footsteps as he made his way down the hall to join us in the kitchen. Everyone was in much better spirits this morning, all happily going about the morning.

"Do you want me to put your hair up for you, Esmari?" Mom asked. I nodded, and she got right to work as I bit into my muffin. Mom smoothed my hair and tied it into a high ponytail. "There, now it will be out of your face."

Bray came in and leaned over top of me, taking my juice. "Mornin'!" He smiled.

"Bray!" I whined, but it was too late. He had already taken a big gulp of what was supposed to be my glass of orange juice and plopped down next to Dad.

"Here, I already had some at home," Hunter said sliding, his juice to me. I stuck my tongue out at Bray and he made a silly face at me, making me almost spit out my drink. There was a rhythmic knock on the back door. Mom smoothed her apron and went to answer it.

"Oh! Good morning!" Mom greeted enthusiastically. I glanced over to see Maya and Corbin entering. "Please come in and help yourself to a fresh muffin."

"Thank you," Maya said.

A tinging timer went off, and Mom rushed to retrieve the last of the muffins from the oven. She switched it off and placed the pan on a hot pad nearby. Maya and Corbin both took a blueberry treat and leaned against the nearby wall.

"Wow!" Corbin exclaimed, enthralled in the blueberry muffin, now half crumbling apart in his hands.

"I know, right?" Said Hunter. I smiled and watched Maya eat her muffin gracefully.

We all chatted about little things like the

weather and whatnot. Mom fussed over my hair a little more, brushing the ponytail over and over. I took the moment in, realizing that this was the last time we would all be together at the table laughing like this, without a care in the world. Time seemed to slow down for just a moment as I tried my best to remember every detail of the scene. Every crumb on Bray's mouth. Every last detail of my dad's smile when he gazed upon my mom. The sound of my mom's laughter as she chatted with Maya. And of course, Hunter's giddy look on his face as he and Corbin dug into another blueberry muffin.

Maya was soon urging us to head out. I wanted to capture the moment forever, but I also knew that it was time to go. Mom got my bag from my room and handed it to me.

"Be safe, sweetie," she said with tears in her eyes. She gave a great big hug and held on tight. Finally, she kissed my cheek and backed away, dabbing the tears from her cheeks with her fingertips.

"You have everything?" Dad asked. I nodded. "Okay, well, remember, we are always here. And don't forget to write, for your Mother's sake, and mine."

"Hang on, before you leave!" Bray said, running out of the room. He came back a moment later with a small peanut butter jar-shaped enamel pin in his hand. I had saved up and bought it for him for his birthday one year. Mom and Dad never understood why I was so adamant on getting him that particular pin. Bray fastened it to the front of my bag. "If you ever need it," he said and winked at me. He sighed and pulled me in for a big bear hug.

"Bye, Bray," I mumbled into his chest.

"Be careful, sis," he whispered. He released me and turned to Hunter. "You take care of her, Hunter."

Hunter nodded nervously. "I will, I promise."

The four of us left the house, Maya and Corbin leading the way. We walk out to the edge of town. Hunter and I glanced back at our hometown. I felt as if someone was shutting a book on this part of my life. I smiled at Hunter, who looked nervous for the first time about the trip. I think it set in for him, too. He took a big sigh and linked arms with me. He nodded to me. Maya and Corbin paused just ahead of us.

"Ready for our adventure?" Hunter asked, sticking his nose in the air.

I pursed my lips and gave a sharp nod. Hunter grinned, and we took a few strides to catch up with Maya and Corbin. Corbin chuckled at us, then turned to Maya to lead the way. The sun was beaming down on us, and the red dust from the path clouded our feet as we walked. Maya seemed tense as we grew further from the town. We rounded a corner, and the distinguished path grew faint and more over-taken by small weeds, until suddenly, Maya stopped. She handed her small bag to Corbin, and he stepped back.

Maya looked around her for a moment then folded her hands in front of her. I glanced at her face. She closed her eyes as if preparing for something. She slowed her breathing, bringing her arms straight out to the sides of her. It looked as if she was suspended in time. She allowed her hands to float up slowly with her breath, and then, with a quick sharp movement, she threw her hands straight down in front of her as if slamming her palms on a table. A zap sounded off, and a bright gaping hole appeared in the air in front of her.

"Come on," Corbin said. He walked straight into the hole without hesitation.

Hunter hurried after him, and I followed at his heels. It was an odd sensation when I went through, almost like static, making the little hairs on my neck tingle. I blinked, and suddenly I was somewhere completely new. There was soft long grass at my feet. I looked around and saw a massive meadow. I had never seen so much green grass and flowers in one place before. It was breathtaking. Maya stepped through behind me, and the hole vanished. She pressed a finger to her temple and furrowed her eyebrows. Corbin came to her and placed a hand on her shoulder. She calmed her expression and gave him a soft smile.

"Let's take a rest here for a few minutes." Corbin decided, gesturing for us to sit.

Maya carefully sat down and then looked at me. "I'm sure you have questions."

"Yeah, a few," I said. *Where do I begin?*

"Well, let's have it," Maya prompted.

"Are Royals really only women?"

"Ha!" Maya laughed. "Interesting first question. No, in fact, they are not. Royals can be men or women. They often come from a Royal bloodline, but, every so often, a Royal comes from a Non-Royal family, like you. And they always have the mark."

"What mark?" Hunter whispered under his breath.

"Don't strain yourself, only they can see it." Corbin chuckled.

"What about 'the power' that Royals have?" I asked.

Maya's eyes twinkled with amusement. "Well, every Royal has something that is their special 'power' for lack of better name. I think it sounds ridiculous to call it this, but hey, I didn't name it. Anyway, I, for example, have the power of

Pathfinding. I can create pathways or portals, like the one we just stepped through to hop from place to place."

"She can't just pick anywhere in the world to go, however," Corbin chimed in. "There are limitations on how far we can portal hop."

"Right, like Corbin said. Take today. To get from Athra to Banshui, your new home, I can't just do one portal to get us there. It's way too far, and my body and abilities can't handle that. So, instead, it will take three, maybe four, pathways," Maya explained.

"And she has to be mindful of her body and take a rest after making a pathway if she needs to," Corbin said. It was almost more of a cheeky reminder to Maya than it was information for us.

"Yes, yes," Maya said. It was the most childish and playful I had heard her sound. "Alright, let's get going again."

We stood and followed Maya a bit further in the grassy meadow. When she found the right spot, we stopped, and she began the same way as before. She folded her hands in front of her and closed her eyes. She slowed her breathing and brought her arms out to her sides. Then she allowed them to float up just before jolting her hands straight down. It was just as mesmerizing as the first time. We all made our way through the portal, this time ending up in a clearing in what appeared to be a forest.

"Three," Maya said to Corbin. "I think we can do it in three."

"Okay, don't push it. If we need to have another rest stop, we can. Plus, if I'm not mistaken, those two are enjoying the journey," Corbin said, pointing at Hunter and me.

It was true. We had never seen trees so tall before. And the sounds from different creatures around us was incredible. There was something almost eerie about this place from the way the mist made each beam of sunlight look coming through the trees. It was beautiful and mystical. Almost mysterious. Maya and Corbin sat on a fallen tree while Hunter and I stayed standing.

"Maya," I started.

"More questions?" She smiled. Her eyes looked more tired now.

"How did you know that you could Pathfind?" I asked.

She thought for a moment. "Well, my mom also had the Pathfinding ability. Abilities, sorry, I mean powers, are often passed down from a parent. But one day, when I had just gotten my wings, I was throwing a fit about who knows what. I was slamming my hands down over and over with frustration. I remember thinking about wanting to be outside. And then, suddenly, there I was. I had, at some point, created a Pathway, and somehow managed to go through, unknowingly," she laughed and shook her head. The charms in her hair clicked together to the rhythm of her laughter. "I gave my parents such a scare. Myself too. But, over time, I learned how it worked."

"Huh," I said with a deep huff.

"A power could be so many things, so it may be difficult to pinpoint what yours is. Being that you didn't come from Royal parents, you won't have a base idea of what it could be." Maya said, standing. "The last leg of our trip awaits."

Maya again created a pathway. And we all ventured through one by one, Maya again coming through last. Maya looked exhausted, sitting on the ground as soon as she was through. Corbin sat to her back and prompted her to lean against him for a moment. He was calm about it, with no sense of urgency in his actions. *He is probably used to seeing her like this.*

Hunter and I looked around us. We seemed to be in another meadow-like area. The grass here was thinner and softer than the one before. Little yellow dandelions were sprinkled all around us. In the distance, I could see a hill with a stone archway near the top. The sun was overhead and beating down warmth on us. I could hear a whooshing sound somewhere nearby. A cool, humid breeze surrounded us as we took in the sight, making the air smell sweet.

Maya took a big whiff. "Ah. Smells like home." She smiled. The rest seemed to do her well, and she looked like some of her energy was back. She and Corbin stood and glanced at us. "Ready?"

I nodded, and before I could blink, she started to flutter above the ground. Her wings glistened in the sunlight. Corbin followed, with Hunter and I behind him. His wings reminded me of gray smoke the way they moved. Maya headed toward the stone archway. My heart pounded with excitement. As we grew closer, I could hear the once distant whooshing sound growing louder. *It sounds like water.* We stayed close to the ground as we fluttered up the slight hill. The breeze from our wings made the grass sway beneath us. We passed just through the archway and landed on the ground.

I shielded my eyes from the sunlight and gasped as I took in the sight. There were buildings and homes spread out as far as the eye could see, all of beautiful, stone textures. Some buildings were on the ground, while others were in the sky at varying heights. A large building towered over several structures near it with an intricate moving sculpture standing at its peak. The pathways were made of detailed brickwork leading to different areas of the town. And at the far right, I could see a small sliver of beachfront, with waves crashing against the sand and rocks. There were weeping willow trees all over on the surface level, providing shade and greenery among all the stone and brickwork.

"Welcome to Banshui," Maya whispered to me.

I could hear children laughing and playing somewhere nearby as we strolled our way towards the buildings. I was in complete awe. There seemed to be different groupings of homes and buildings, all different by small characteristics. The town was bustling with people who all looked content to be here. I looked at Hunter, who was as wide-eyed as I was. Corbin and Maya looked less in awe and more relieved and at peace to be home. As excited as I was, I suddenly felt so very far from home. This town was much larger than Athra, with so many more people here. I felt lost and out of place. I looked at my feet, each step suddenly more daunting than the last.

What if I'm not who they think I am? What if I really don't belong here? I was so lost in thought, I didn't even notice Hunter had come to a complete stop, right in front of me. I walked straight into him, sending both of us crashing to the ground.

"Ouch!" Hunter mumbled. He got up and

brushed off.

I sat for a moment, getting my bearings again. I placed my hands in the grass and stabilized myself. "Sorry, I—" My mind went blank. *Small boy. He's kicked a ball too hard*—I jumped to my feet and leaped in front of Corbin, reaching out my hands. "Watch out!" I gasped as I felt the sting of the rubber ball bounce off my palms.

The little boy came running over from behind some trees. "Sorry!" He called, grabbing his ball and going back over with his friends again. They ran off, back to a small clearing behind the trees, and began to play again.

Maya looked at me as if she were analyzing me all over again. She seemed deep in thought and didn't say a word. She glanced off toward where the boy had gone and then back at me. She walked to where I was sitting on the ground and crouched. Again, she looked off toward the trees and then looked where I was. Finally, she stood looking at the ground and smirked with her arms folded.

"Let's go to Agathin, let her know we all arrived safely," Maya said as she set off.

Maya led us into the bustle of the town where there were little shops and cafes. It reminded me of Sky Athra, in a way, with the variety and uniqueness strewn about. It felt upscale. I admired the different window displays as we passed the boutiques. Many people were staring as the four of us walked by, some whispering to one another. I felt awkward and self-conscious, finding myself tugging at the hem of my shirt. Most people were dressed more sophisticated in this town, and I definitely didn't fit in with my dusty shoes and casual clothing.

We entered a small building that just had the word "AFFAIRS OFFICE" in large letters on the wall. Maya pulled a small red string by the wall that sounded off a low buzz sound. After a few moments, an older woman with short, curly, silver hair came from behind the tall tinted glass door.

"Ah! Binbin, Maya! Welcome back!" she said. Her voice sounded very familiar.

"Binbin?" Hunter whispered to me. I looked at him and shrugged.

"Come in, come in," said the woman, leading us back behind the door. The environment was simple but cozy. A complete change from just outside these walls. We made our way to a seating area and all relaxed onto the various brown leather sofas and chairs. The woman looked at me. "I see you found her."

"Agathin, this is Esmari and her friend Hunter," said Corbin.

"Hello. It has been a while since we had a Royal from outside of Banshui. Where are you from, Esmari?" Agathin asked.

I looked at Maya, and she nodded in reassurance. "I'm from Athra."

"Oh! Interesting. I had it wrong, didn't I, Maya?" Agathin chuckled. Her short stature adjusted in the chair next to mine as she fixed her hand-embroidered burgundy colored shawl on her shoulders. *She was the voice I heard when I was learning to fly!* "Either I am losing my touch, or—ah well, you are here now. I don't believe we have had a Royal from Athra before!"

I smiled nervously. Hunter nudged me and smiled with pride. The fan across the room kicked on, sending a chill down my spine.

"Well, I officially welcome you to Banshui. We are a town of both Royals and Non-Royals. You will find that many of us have grown up here, many are children or grandchildren, and so forth of Royals or their Accompanying. This is a place that you can feel safe and learn your place as a Royal. A lot of shops, and such, are owned by Non-Royals, but occasionally, a Royal finds their power useful in less glamorous tasks. Like for instance, our little bakery shop in town is managed by a Royal whose power is a form of Needs power. He automatically knows the perfect treat you should have according to your mood and taste buds. It's really quite something!" Agathin rambled.

"What is your power?" I asked.

"Well, dear, I have the Finding power. My particular power allows me to find Royals when they get their wings. Sometimes, even before. Because of this, I also help manage the placement of new Royals, such as yourself," Agathin explained. "Your power will help begin to determine where you fit. And we can place you with mentors in your field of power to help you learn how exactly your power works. So, Esmari, do you happen to know of your power? Something that happens or that you make happen, but don't know why?"

Before I had a chance to think, Maya spoke up. "Actually, Agathin, I think she may have some kind of Sight power," Maya stated.

"Interesting. Why do you think that?" Agathin asked, thoroughly intrigued.

"As we came into town, Esmari jumped out to stop a ball from hitting Corbin," Maya started to explain, then looked at me.

"I just saw the kid kick the ball too hard, and it was headed straight for him," I said uncomfortably. *Why does it feel like what I did is wrong?*

"From where you were at, I have no idea how you saw the ball coming at him, let alone that a kid kicked that ball," Maya said calmly. "Has that ever happened before?"

"Yeah!" Hunter blurted out. "The day you were learning to fly. After we raced, Es asked, 'Why is Bray here?' Bray is her brother and—right, right, besides the point— what I'm getting at is it Bray was, like, *way* far away at the time. I didn't even see him. I thought it was odd at the time, but kind of forgot about it until now."

Agathin was nodding and looked like she was carefully considering the information. She seemed pleased. She stroked at her chin with a wrinkled, pale hand and nodded again. It was as if she was having a silent conversation with herself. I watched feeling almost embarrassed about these things that happened. *Do I tell them about the other times? I don't even know for sure what happened. How was I going to tell them if I wasn't even sure?*

"It would be the first with Sight in a while." Agathin smiled, thinking aloud. She turned to Maya. "I only know of one person who teaches in Sight power. I'll give him a ring later today and inform him that we will need him."

"Okay," Maya said, standing. "Well, if there isn't anything more—"

"Maya, I know this is not usually your jurisdiction, but we need to get them settled. I have a place set up for Esmari, a room in the dorms. There should be an envelope set aside with my name on it when you get there. And as for Hunter, if you don't mind, Binbin, could you help him find a room at the Accompanying dorms. I know we had a few young men move out recently, so there should be some vacancy," Agathin said. Maya seemed hesitant at first but nodded in agreement. "Thank you. Usually, I help, or my assistant, but, being that she is gone today, I can't leave this place unattended. Plus, I have a meeting soon that I have to attend to."

Corbin smiled sincerely. "We will get them settled for you."

"Wonderful. Tomorrow morning, Esmari, you will need to check in with the Head of Academy. He is expecting you and will help you connect with your teacher. The academy is filled with others learning their abilities just like you. Hunter, you will also have some courses available to you to learn different skills and maybe find a trait you would like to pursue. You both will have all of your necessities available to you at the dorms, but reach out if there is something missing," Agathin instructed. We all stood, and she led us out to the front doors. She reached out and laid a hand on my arm. "Esmari, I realize that this all may be overwhelming, but I'm sure you will find your footing. You're strong. I can tell that already. There are plenty of people around to offer help, though, if you need it. Please come back and visit me anytime you would like to."

"Thank you," I sighed.

We all exited the building and began making our way down the street toward the large building we had seen before, passing a few more clothing shops and two cafes along the way. I admired the moving sculpture again as we drew near. A shop in the sky cast its shadow down on us, like a cloud passing the sun. Metal lettering on the face of the ash-gray stone building read "Academy." We paused out front giving me a moment to get my sense of direction again. There was a small cluster of two-story buildings just to the right of the academy. To the left was a large empty lot with similar two-story buildings in the distance.

"This is the academy that Agathin was telling you about. Just over there are the dorms where you will be staying," Maya said, pointing to the cluster of buildings. "And Hunter will be at those down the way."

"Cool! Gives us a good midway point to find each other while we get used to the area, right, Es?" Hunter said. His eyes were twinkling with excitement.

"Corbin, please show Hunter where to go," Maya said.

"Meet here just after sundown?" I asked

quickly. Hunter smiled with a big grin and nodded.

We all parted ways. Maya and I made our way to my new dorm. There was a group of three buildings all facing each other and connected by a round courtyard with several picnic benches and more weeping willow trees strewn about. We entered the one to the right labeled, "Building B," and found a small envelope at the desk just inside the corridor with Agathin's name scribbled on the front. Inside were a golden key and paper map of the dorms. The room with the number 47 was circled. Maya handed me the key and map and pointed me in the right direction.

"Here we are. There are two floors. Floor one has rooms 1-29, and floor two has 30-49. There are multiple lounges and kitchen spaces spread throughout that you can use as well as laundry areas. Someone will get in touch with you to provide you with some clothing. Do you think you can handle it from here?" Maya asked.

"Yeah, I think I can handle it." I smiled.

"Great," Maya said, laying a hand on my shoulder. Her eyes were soft as she smiled at me. "I'll be around."

Maya exited the building, her shoes clicking against the tile floor as she went. I took a breath and looked at the map again to get a better understanding of the building's layout. I suddenly realized how alone I felt. The corridor I was standing in felt like it was growing bigger and bigger, and I was shrinking smaller and smaller. *Okay, Esmari. You can do this. One step at a time.*

I found my way to the staircase closest to my dorm. Natural light from the window shone on the tile flooring. Large abstract pictures were lining the walls on the sides of the stairs, all of calming colors, helping me feel a bit at ease. At the top of the stairs, there were white doors lining both sides of the hall, all looking so similar to each other, aside from a small number plate. I looked down the way and could see breaks every couple of doorways where the kitchen or lounge areas were that Maya had mentioned. For a moment, I took another look at the map in my hands, then headed towards my dorm. I passed a lounge area where a few people were relaxing. Some whispers arose as I walked by. I glanced at the map again in hopes that I hadn't gone the wrong way.

A thin, tall, feminine figure stepped right in front of me, making me jump. "Are you lost?" She said, her high voice laced with fake concern. Her long, curled brown hair sat perfectly draped over one shoulder. She was dressed elegantly and sleek. Everything about her, from the smirk of her glossed lips, to the way she stood high and mighty, made me irritated.

"No, I'm just finding my dorm," I said, pursing my lips into a cold smile.

"Oh! You're new?" she said. It was clearly not a question I needed to answer. *Obviously, I'm new.* Fighting the urge to roll my eyes at her, I nodded anyway. She looked me over with her green eyes, "So, what crown do you wear?"

Crown? Was she serious? Only Royalty in fairy tales wore crowns. "What? Do you want to polish it for me?" I said, matching her fake tone.

A tall male lounging on one of the chairs nearby snickered quietly. His back was to me, but he turned for a moment showing the profile of his face as he glanced at the two of us. His sharp features were striking and handsome. He turned back to his book, making the deep burgundy tones of his very dark brown hair dance in the light. The girl scoffed and rolled her eyes at me shifting her weight.

"You—" she started, looking sour.

Someone threw a dainty arm over my shoulder. "There you are!" announced the feminine, upbeat voiced person, now hanging off of my shoulder.

I looked over to see a girl about my age with bright blue eyes. She tucked her shoulder-length hair behind her ear and grinned at me. I admired how her hair faded from a bright blonde to an orange-red color at the ends.

"Hi," I smiled back as friendly as I could.

"Well, see ya!" said the blonde-haired girl, waving as she ushered me away.

I looked back to the girl we left in the lounge area rolling her eyes and letting out a great big sigh in our direction. She turned with her nose in the air and went towards a chair. We stopped abruptly at a door numbered 46, and the blonde-haired girl let go of my shoulders. She stepped back and shoved a hand in her jeans pocket, pulling out a key.

"She just—Ug!" grunted the girl. She smoothed my shirt sleeves for me. "Sorry about that! You must be new around here. I'm Jewelei. Most people call me Jewel or Jewels. That was Belleza. Trust me when I say you don't want to be her friend."

"Definitely not," I said under my breath.

"She just thinks that she is so much better than everyone else," Jewel continued, crinkling her nose in disgust. She paused, calming herself. "Anyway, you need help finding your dorm?"

"Actually, I think that one is mine," I said, pointing at the next door over with the number 47 on it.

"No way! That room has been empty for so long! I like you already. How neat that we will be neighbors, too! This is going to be so fun!" Jewel squealed. "You go settle in and then come over to my dorm when you are done!"

"Sure. That would be nice," I said. I felt a warmth inside of me melting away some of the loneliness I was feeling.

Jewels entered her dorm, and I went to mine. I inserted the key, and the door clicked open. Inside, the room smelled of fresh-cut flowers. It was a larger dorm room than I expected. A shine reflected off of the freshly polished dark wood flooring. There was a small fridge that I opened to find stocked with various drinks and produce. On top was a basket full of other foods with a note that read, "I hope you enjoy these snacks while settling in! -Agathin."

I hung my bag on the metal hook behind the door. Across the room was a light wood-framed bed against the cream-colored wall and a comfy looking chair next to the window with a simple floor lamp beside it. Next to an almost empty bookcase sat a white desk with a corded telephone just at the foot of the bed. I had my own small bathroom already equip with everything I was going to need, as well as a small walk-in closet with some clothes hung inside. Right in the center of the space was a big fluffy round white rug, which wasn't really my style, but I liked the warmth it brought to the room.

While it had everything I needed, the room seemed empty and plain. It was far from what I was used to seeing every morning when I woke up. *New room, new adventure, new Esmari.* Smiling at my own reassurance, I took out the journal from my backpack and placed it on the desk. It was the start of making this space feel like my own.

I decided to go over to Jewel's room. I knocked gently on the door, and, a moment later, she swung it open eagerly. The room was filled with personality. It was colorful and inviting and so striking after being inside my plain room. Jewel's face was beaming with happiness and life.

"Come in, come in!" She welcomed with excitement. She closed the door behind me. "I realized I introduced myself earlier and never asked your name! How ignorant of me!"

"It's okay," I smiled. "I'm Esmari."

"Well, Esmari, make yourself at home! Want something to drink? I just got some new juice drinks?" She called, ducking her head to look into her little mint colored fridge.

"Sure, thanks," I called back, taking a seat in a large blue beanbag chair. She brought me a small bottle of juice and plopped down in the other beanbag chair beside me.

"So," she said, taking a big gulp of her beverage. "What district are you from?"

"District?" I repeated, feeling stupid.

"Yeah, you know, district. I'm from the West District of Banshui. This is Central District here. So, which are you from?" She asked.

"Um, I'm not from a district," I said, looking at my hands.

"Everyone in Banshui is from a district!" Jewel laughed. She adjusted the neck of her green T-shirt.

"No, I'm not from Banshui. I'm from Athra," I explained. A feeling of embarrassment crept up inside of me.

"Whoa. Not from Banshui? That's crazy! There hasn't been an outsider for forever. And a Royal! Wait, you are a Royal, right?" She paused, then smiled and shook her head at herself. "Of course, you're a Royal, you're living in these dorms, you have to be."

"So, what's the deal with Belleza?" I asked, changing the subject.

Jewel scrunched her nose and sighed. "She's one of the popular girls at the academy, and I think it has seriously gone to her head. She's from my district, and she's always been like that. Though, she was kind of brought up that way. Her parents are important figures and make good money."

"Ah," I said.

"What's your Athra like?" Jewel asked, her eyes glistening with wonder.

"Nothing like Banshui. It's so much smaller. We have two sections, Sky Athra and Athra. But, we don't have those, um, district things," I told her. "I'm a bit nervous that I will get lost here, to be honest."

"Oh, well, don't worry about that! I've grown up in Banshui, and I came to the Central District a lot, so I won't let you get lost! It's pretty cool around here, lots to see."

"Hey, Jewel, can I ask you something?" I started.

"Sure! Anything," she smiled.

"Earlier, Belleza asked me something about a crown. What was that all about?" I asked sheepishly. *Please, don't laugh at me.*

"Oh, right, you wouldn't know that term. It, well," she paused to think. "It's sort of a way to figure out how Royal you are based on your parents. It's ridiculous, but some people think it makes them more important Royals. Completely untrue, of course. There are three categories. I'm a broken crown because I only have one Royal parent."

"Both of my parents aren't Royal, so what does that make me?" I asked.

"Someone with no Royal parents is called a dirt head. And then, there's people whose parents are both Royal. Those people are called solid crowns. Belleza is a solid crown and only will befriend solid crowns. So, anyone you ever see with her are solid crowns, too. I think she really believes that she wears a shiny crown on her head some days," Jewel said, rolling her eyes. She sat up tall and pretended to place a crown on her head and stuck her nose way up in the sky. I giggled at her silly display. She relaxed back and accidentally bumped the juice bottle against her leg, spilling what was left in the bottle on the floor. "Ah, man!"

"Oh, I'll get you something to clean it up!" I gasped.

"No worries. I've got it," she said, crouching next to the spill. Instead of getting a nearby napkin, she reached down with her hand and scooped up the liquid like it was a piece of putty. I couldn't believe my eyes. She stood and carried it over to her bathroom sink, then placed it inside. The juice ran down the sink, and she brushed off the excess drops before wiping her hand on a hand towel.

"How did—" I stuttered.

She laughed. "Right, you probably aren't used to seeing people's power abilities. My ability is in the Water category. It's really nothing more than what you saw. I can play with liquid as if it were dough in my hands."

"Cool," I said. I looked out the window, realizing how much time had passed. The sun was beginning to set, putting an orange glow over everything outside. "Shoot! I'm supposed to meet my friend in a bit."

"Oh, okay," Jewel said as I stood up. There was a tinge of disappointment in her voice.

"Do you want to come with? You'd like Hunter. Maybe you can show us around a bit?" I blurted with excitement.

"Yeah! Oh, and I know just the place to take you guys. You will love it!" Jewel said, nearly jumping with joy.

Jewel and I met Hunter in front of the school. He was twirling a small twig between his fingers, looking like he had been waiting a while. When he saw us, his face lit up. He tossed his twig on the ground and smoothed his shirt down. He stood tall, and he strolled over to us in a sophisticated manner. It seemed out of character for him.

"Hello," Hunter greeted, bowing his head slightly.

"Hey, Hunter. What's with the walk and the bow?" I asked.

"I, uh, hem," he stuttered, clearing his throat. "I'm in the presence of Royalty."

"Knock it off." I laughed, nudging him playfully. "Hunter, this is Jewelei."

"Call me Jewel or Jewels. None of the Jewelei. Too formal," she shrugged.

"Hunter is my best friend from Athra. He's a goofball, but he's a nice guy," I explained to Jewel. "Alright, you lead the way, Jewel!"

"Okay, friends! Since you're not familiar with the place, I'll try to explain as we go. First, this is, of course, the academy. Esmari, this is likely where you were told to go already, yes?" Jewel said.

"Yes, I'm supposed to meet the Head of the Academy tomorrow morning," I explained.

"Ah! You'll be meeting Mr. Higgens. He's quite the Royal! And he's been the Head for who knows how long. Hunter, you on the other hand, won't be coming here tomorrow, were you told that?"

"Yes," Hunter said. "I'm joining classes at the Center."

"Good. Okay, now that way is what we call the Square. Though it's not really square, come to think of it. It's where lots of the hustle and bustle of Central District is. Lots of fancy shops and businesses. Induction Affairs office is down that way, too. A lady named Agathin is in charge of it. She's supposedly a Finder. She knows and helps keep track of who's who of all the Royals," Jewel's voice trailed off in amazement for a moment.

"She's really nice, actually. We met her," I noted.

"You what! You mean to tell me you actually

met Agathin herself?" Jewel gasped. I nodded. She thought for a moment. "I guess it makes sense. You don't have family from here, so you would have to go there. That's so cool, though. Not a lot of people from Banshui actually meet her. She's kind of like a legend."

"I'll take you to meet her sometime," I said.

"Well, look at you. You've been here, what? A day? And you are going to introduce me to people!" Jewel laughed, sticking her hands on her hips. "Anyway, there are lots of places over in the Square, but I want to show you two my favorite spot to go to. It's over this way, just inside what's called the Coastal District."

Jewel stepped back and opened her delicate, iridescent, almost clear wings. She fluttered into the sky, and we followed just as the last bit of light left, revealing the night's beautiful stars. There was a glow from the square as the shops and businesses lit up their multitude of signs. Out ahead, there was a twinkling of soft lights from some small homes and quaint businesses. As we passed into the Coastal District, the entire ambiance changed. We headed for a small business that was floating in the sky overlooking the shoreline in the near distance.

We landed on a rustic style porch, just in front of the entry. A sign swinging overhead read, "The

Dripping Crown." Jewel opened the door chiming a small bell as we entered. Inside was relaxing with the low lights and occasional water feature. There were sofas and chairs off to the left and a countertop bar with a couple of seats in front of us. To our right was a small staircase leading up to a loft. Strewn all over the walls were all sorts of abstract photographs. A man a few years our senior with a charcoal gray flat cap on looked up at us from behind the counter. Adjusting his wire-rimmed glasses, he tossed the towel in his hand at the sink.

"Jewels!" he called. His carrot-colored goatee gleamed below his genuine smile.

"It's quiet in here tonight," Jewel noted. Looking around at the empty chairs.

"Yeah, well," he shrugged. "I see you brought some new faces!"

"Vic, this is Esmari and Hunter. They are new in town. Esmari, Hunter, this is Victor. The owner of The Dripping Crown," Jewel introduced.

Victor shook our hands heartily. "Royal?" he said, pointing at me. I nodded. "So, you're new in town? Where are you two from?"

"Athra." I smiled.

"Whoa. That's quite some distance! Well, welcome to Banshui. Have you had any dinner?" Victor asked.

"Not yet, Vic," Jewel answered with a hopeful smile.

"Alright, I'll fix you up some sandwiches," Victor chuckled, heading back behind the counter. "It's on me tonight! What are you all drinking?"

I looked up at the menu. There were all kinds of coffees and teas, many I hadn't tried before, let alone ever heard of. Beside the list of teas, there was a list of smoothies of every fruit you could think of, as well as milkshake flavors. I felt overwhelmed by the options at hand, but finally decided to try something called a Zebra Mocha. We gave our orders to Victor, and he got to work.

"Goin' up?" Victor said, motioning to the stairs.

"Yup," Jewel said.

We headed up the creaking staircase to a cozy loft. Big windows to the side looked out to the crashing waves on the beach. There was a window seat decorated with striped pillows where Jewel plopped down. Hunter sat on a floor cushion against the railing overlooking the counter below. I took the opportunity to relax into a hanging hammock chair facing the windows. A delicious aroma rose up into the loft as Victor came to deliver our sandwiches and drinks. He plopped down next to Jewel and took a sip out of a mug.

"So, Hunter, did you get settled okay?" I asked

as I adjusted the sleeve of the warm coffee drink in my hand.

"Mmmhmm," he mumbled through a mouthful of what Victor called an artichoke heart sandwich. He took a big swallow. "Yeah. I'm sharing a dorm with another guy. He seems nice. I met some of the other guys in the dorms, too. They showed me around the dorms a bit so I'd know where to find everything. We even have a phone in the dorm. I guess the extension is the dorm number. Mine's number ten."

"Yeah, I saw one in my dorm, too. I'm dorm number forty-seven," I said, reaching for a wedge of the grilled turkey and tomato melt I had been waiting to cool down.

"Forty- seven. I'll try to remember that," Hunter said. He took another bite of sandwich. "Man, this is so good!"

Victor chuckled. "Glad you like it!"

"There's a couple other coffee joints around, but Vic has the best one, I think. Plus, he serves delicious food, and some of the other ones don't serve food at all," Jewel praised. "I've been coming here for forever. Ever since I got my wings. I even help out every so often when it gets busy. I'm not too great at the food yet, but Vic has taught me how to make most of the drinks. Just last week I learned how to properly steam the milk."

"Yeah, you've picked it up pretty well," Victor noted.

I smiled as I took in the moment of peace. It was the most relaxed I had felt since I had made the decision to come to Banshui. I felt comfortable. Maybe it was the cozy environment of the loft, or maybe the light conversations we were having, but I felt at ease. I didn't feel so lost. I didn't feel out of place. I felt reassured in my decision. I felt hope.

eight

Early the next morning, I woke to the sun shining into my window and lighting up my dorm in a beautiful hue of gold. I got up and dressed in a spare shirt and pants that were hung in my closet just as my phone rang. The lady on the other end informed me to come by her shop later that evening to pick out some clothing in my style. I thanked her and hung up, finding myself feeling excited to get some new clothing. *The new Esmari.* I smiled to myself and left the room, bumping into Jewel in the hall.

"Well, good morning!" she said. "I was hoping I'd run into you! I thought that you might want a buddy to walk to the academy with this morning. Being your first day and all! You nervous?"

I thought for a moment. "Anxious, I think."

"Ah, well. That's a good way to look at it!" Jewel linked her arm in mine, and we started for the academy.

As we entered the towering double doors into the echoing tile-floored lobby of the academy, my heart began to pound. The bang of the door behind us made me jolt. The walls of the lobby were tall and plastered with plaques of different shapes and styles, boasting of the academy's many achievements. A large bronze chandelier hung high in the center of the room. Directly in front of us sat a massive, dooming staircase that made me feel like a small child. To either side was a hallway with the letters "A" and "B" presented boldly on the wall to their side.

"Okay, Mr. Higgens' office is just up the staircase to the right. Look for the red door all the way at the end. You can't miss it," Jewel said, unlinking from my now trembling arm.

I eyed the taupe wall just to the top of the

staircase where large, scripty letters were painted in charcoal gray. "Professor Javion's Academy for Royalty," I read aloud.

Jewel nodded. "Yup. The founder of the academy. Professor Javion. I don't know much about him, just that his name is on the wall," she said with a shrug, her voice echoing in the barren lobby. "Most of us just call this place the academy, mainly because saying the full name is quite the mouthful."

"Why is it so empty in here?" I asked suddenly.

"Different teachers hold classes at different times. I have an open lab time today. Those aren't mandatory. It's usually busier later in the day," Jewel reassured. "I'll see you later."

I waved her goodbye as she headed down hall "B" and took a big shaky breath. A sudden wave of fear washed over me. Everything happened so fast over the past few days that I was waiting for someone to tell me this all was a big joke. Maybe I'd walk into that office, and they'd tell me that I really didn't belong here after all. That there had been some big misunderstanding. They'd arrange to take me back to Athra as soon as possible. Probably make me sign something promising to never disclose information about Banshui, and then leave me to live my boring normal life in peace. I sighed and shook my head, feeling conflicting emotions growing more unsettling by the moment. *Just have to take the first step, Es.*

Slowly, I started my climb up the deep espresso-colored wooden planks of the staircase, each step feeling more unsettling than the last. I veered down the long hallway. There were doors on either side of me, but just as Jewel said, at the very end of the hall was a single vibrant red door. Raising a still trembling hand to the door, I gave it a gentle knock.

"Enter!" said a deep voice.

I twisted the doorknob, and the latch clicked open with a small metallic ting sound. My nostrils were met by a sweet cinnamon scent as I took in the scenery now surrounding me. The room had a cozy feel to the ambiance. A large dark wooden desk sat centered in front of the tall windows that flooded the room with natural light. The entire wall to my left was a great big bookshelf stuffed with books of all kinds, along with the occasional dainty artistic sculpture. An older gentleman with dark skin and curly short gray hair was leaned against the wall to the right, patiently watching as I took in the environment before me. His eyes met mine as I stepped away from the doorway and closed the door. He smiled, adjusted the intricately carved cane in his left hand, and motioned me toward one of the large black leather armchairs sitting just in front of the desk.

"Esmari, I presume," he said. "Please, come take a seat."

"Thank you," I said, trying to hide the nervous tone in my voice.

He stepped toward the desk, smoothing down the front of his navy-blue suit jacket. I took a seat and glanced at a slouched, messy-looking man in the chair next to me. The desk held a nameplate that read "MR. HIGGENS" in bold silver lettering, next to a small moving sculpture that clicked as it rocked.

"Welcome to Professor Javion's Academy for Royalty. My name is Mr. Higgens," the man with the cane said, waving toward the nameplate. "I am the Head of the Academy. I spoke with Agathin, and she tells me you are from Athra, yes?"

"Yes, sir. I just arrived yesterday." I nodded.

"I hope you find a liking to our Banshui. Likewise, I hope you can find a liking to this academy. This academy is a place to help you not only discover your abilities, but to learn and make mistakes along the way. You will get out of it what effort you put in, and I hope you will put in the time and effort. I am told you have a sort of Sight power. This will be your instructor," Mr. Higgens said, nodding toward the messy looking man next to me. "Quite unlike lots of the other powers, you will be the only student studying this ability category at this time. And Mr. Sean, here, is the only teacher we have in this department. I do hope you two can work well together." Mr. Higgens' eyes were no longer on me, but on the man, as if giving him no other option.

Mr. Sean scowled toward Mr. Higgens with a scruffy-bearded face. His icy blue-green eyes glanced at me for a moment and then stared back at Mr. Higgens. He ran a calloused hand through his greasy brown hair before staring down at the scuffed boots on his feet. The tension in the room made my stomach tie in knots. *He clearly didn't volunteer to teach me.* Mr. Sean took a large sigh and stood abruptly, shrugging his long tan trench coat back onto both hunched shoulders. He pinched the bridge of his nose for a moment.

"Let's go. Your lessons will start today. Follow me to your new classroom," Mr. Sean said to me with a gravelly voice. He swung the door open and headed into the hallway without so much as a glance back.

I stood hurriedly, smoothing down my shirt. "Thank you, Mr. Higgens," I said and ran out after Mr. Sean.

Mr. Sean walked swiftly with his head down and his hands shoved in his pockets. I followed him down the stairs and into hall "A" which then split off into three more hallways. Mr. Sean didn't pause, not even for a moment, and he never looked back to make sure I was keeping up. I mentally noted the labels on the hallways as we passed through each one, also taking note of a set of doors labeled "Cafeteria." We weaved through the halls until coming to a dimly lit hall in what seemed to be the back of the academy. At the very end stood a single black door, which we entered through.

"This is the classroom you will be attending each day as I see fit," Mr. Sean grunted.

I stepped inside and was taken aback by the change in scenery. There was a slightly musky smell to the large space. The brick flooring echoed against Mr. Sean's boots as he made his way further into the room. Three tall windows surrounded a built-in platform, casting their light on a podium strategically placed at a slight angle to the opening in the room. In the far back corner of the room, just past the rows of stuffed-full bookshelves, I could see a worn, wooden door propped slightly ajar, leading to what looked like a small private office room for Mr. Sean.

"It is a bit rare to have a Sight power, but don't let that go to your head, thinking you are special or nothin'. These shelves are full of different documents and books to help you learn your specific power. There are some books you aren't going to be ready for and some techniques you won't be trying until I say you are ready. What I say goes. Got that?" Mr. Sean said coarsely.

"Yes, sir," I breathed.

"And another thing, my office is off-limits. If I'm in there and the door is closed, don't bother me," he said, facing me for the first time since we left Mr. Higgens' office. He looked me over, the scowl on his face never changing. Scrunching his eyes shut, he pinched the bridge of his nose while letting out a sigh. "Alright, since you aren't from here, we will be startin' at the basics. You will need to know about the general history and knowledge of Royals before we can even begin on pinpointing the specifics of your ability, let alone strengthening or expandin' it."

Mr. Sean clomped off to a bookshelf, muttering to himself. I stayed put, not really sure what he was wanting me to do. I shifted uncomfortably and glanced around the room again. I could hear him shifting books. A loud bang echoed as he seemed to toss a book to the ground, followed by at least two more. With a grunt, he picked up the books and came into view. He had a small stack of well-used books cradled in his arms and shuffled toward the podium. He slammed them down and retrieved a small, palm-sized notebook from his pocket. Mr.

Sean tore a handful of papers from the notebook and began thumbing through the slew of books, placing the papers in as bookmarks. Without looking up, he lifted a few fingers and motioned me over.

"Read through what I have marked. See that up on the wall," Mr. Sean said, pointing up at a round, numberless clock with gold hands. "When both hands are directly up, pointin' to twelve, you can go to lunch. If you have finished, that is. We will discuss what you have learned later."

Mr. Sean shoved his hands back in his pockets and plodded off without another word. I watched after him, his swaying wings catching my attention. They were a cloudy, white color, but not symmetrical. The bottom of his left wing held the mark of Royalty, but his right wing was missing a part, looking as if it had been burnt, with its uneven, blackened scarring along the bottom edge. A piece of his wing dangled like black string below where it should be. My heart ached. I had never seen someone with such a wing deformity. *What happened to you, Mr. Sean?* He entered his office, leaving the door cracked open. Turning to the podium, I took a look at the daunting stack of books left for me. *Better get to it, Esmari.*

I opened the top book to the page marked and began reading about the ever-evolving categories of powers that Royals could possess. Each ability is something that may or may not be what someone else has had in the past. Working my way down the stack of books, I learned about the origin of Banshui and how there were other Royal towns all around the world, all with completely secret locations to the surrounding towns. The Finders not only kept records on all Royals in their location, but also had record of where other communities of Royals were. One book talked about the importance of the purpose of being a Royal in a peacekeeper position and some of the powers that are useful to pursue the profession.

I had gotten so caught up in reading the different books that, when I glanced to see where the gold hands were on the clock, it was already past twelve. My stomach growled. *One last book, then you can eat.*

I opened the last book in the stack, a large hardcovered book with uneven pages, and found myself rushing through the chapter. It was about a group of people lead by a man named Destimov, who believed Royals possessing certain powers were more important than others. Many of his following were something called "Ex's." which also believed that people who didn't possess powers, Non-Royals, were below them and either needed to serve them or be eradicated.

"The Operation of Royalty Protection, or ORP, was founded in Banshui, and was implemented in Royal communities around the world to seek and put a stop to Destimov's followers. Though many of the original group, including Destimov himself, were killed in a raid launched by the ORP, it is still unknown today just how many of these followers remain," I read aloud.

I closed the book and sighed. *Time for some lunch, finally.* Stepping back from the podium, I looked toward the office door still propped open. It was quiet. I walked softly toward the office door and gave the doorframe a hesitant knock.

"Did you finish?" croaked Mr. Sean. Through the small opening, I could see him sitting in front of his desk on the ground with papers laying all around him.

"Yes, I'm heading to lunch now," I said.

"Yeah, okay," he grunted.

I found my way through the winding halls a bit easier than expected. The delicious smell of food coming from the cafeteria helped. Through the doors, I entered and was genuinely surprised by the sight. It was bright and open inside, so unlike the halls I just came from, with both round and square tables scattered about. Each table set with a simple flower centerpiece. It had a sophisticated feel to the room, like I had entered into a classy restaurant instead of an academy cafeteria. There was such a diversity in the people throughout the room, as well, all chatting in groups as they ate. On both sides of the room, Royals had formed small lines leading to counters where cooks were taking orders. I felt overwhelmed as I glanced around the cafeteria, unsure of how to make my next step. Some people's eyes met mine as I stood frozen just inside the doors, while others simply glanced in my direction. I could hear whispers forming around me. *They're all talking about me.* I bit my bottom lip and took a deep breath. Jewel caught my gaze and came to join me.

"Well, there you are! I was beginning to think you weren't going to come for lunch. I figured I'd wait for you. Thought you might want someone to guide you through how things work here," Jewel said, linking her arm with mine and pulling me toward one of the lines. "Just a tip, this is the best food over here. Alright, now, take a look at the menu posted and choose what you would like them to make you! Oh, and if you want it modified at all, be sure to tell them too— Hi! I want the chicken, thanks!"

A man behind the counter took an empty plate and held his hand above the plate. A moment later, the food appeared, steam and all. He handed Jewel her plate and nodded to me, as if to ask my order.

"Hi, um, I'll have the same, please," I said. I couldn't peel my eyes away from the sight. Again, the man created the food, and then gently, he passed it to me. We took a bottle of juice and a roll of utensils from the end of the counter, and Jewel led us to a small empty table. She and I dug into the perfectly cooked meal.

"So," Jewel said, swallowing hard. "Are the rumors true?"

"What rumors?" I asked. At this point, anything could have been said about me.

"Are you really—you know—" she glanced around, lowering her voice, "a Sight?" The tables around us seemed to hush slightly, but maybe I was just being paranoid.

I nodded. "I guess so."

"Wow. Who's your teacher?" Jewel asked.

"A guy named Mr. Sean. Why?" I said, shoving another bite in my mouth.

"Yikes!" she breathed, glancing down at her juice for a moment before looking back up at me. "I hear he's harsh. Supposedly, his last student was someone he knew. Rumor has it that they had some disagreement, and one day, his student just disappeared. Like, poof! Gone. I guess that Mr. Sean changed after that. Of course, there isn't any proof of what really went down."

"Huh," I sighed.

A familiar voice caught my ear. *Belleza.* I glanced up to see her talking a couple of tables from us and daintily picking at the fruit on her plate. A girl next to her giggled at what Belleza was saying as they both shot glances in my direction. The boy who I had seen in the dorms sat in a chair facing our table. He sat silent, looking deep in thought as he stared at the table.

"Ah, her highness in her natural habitat," Jewel scoffed, nodding at Belleza. "Looks like some of her subjects are missing today."

"Who?" I asked.

Jewel laughed. "Her friends. There are usually a few more that sit at the table with them. See that girl, to her right? That's her bestie, Lilly. They are *both* studying under the same teacher as me. Talk about bad luck on my end. And the guy beside them, that's Kasius. Don't really know much about him. He's pretty quiet. Anyway, there's usually one or two others that sometimes stick around with them, but they must not be here today."

Kasius swiftly stood up. He tossed his drink into a nearby trash can and tucked a hand in his pocket. For a moment, I thought I saw him glance at me from the corner of his eye. Then he strode out of the room. Jewel glanced at the clock up on the wall and began scarfing down the last of her food.

"I gotta head back," she said, standing. "I'll

maybe see you later at the dorms, okay?"

I finished the rest of my food, finding myself waiting until Belleza and Lilly had cleared the room before cleaning up my plate and heading back toward the class. I got lost twice on the way back, but thankfully not for long. I entered the room, and listened for Mr. Sean. The door to his office was still propped slightly ajar. I went to tap on the door.

"I'm back, sir," I said gently, taking a peek inside. *I don't think he has moved since I left.*

"Meet me by the podium," he grunted.

I collected the books I had read in a neat stack and waited for Mr. Sean. He came out of the office, rubbing at his neck as he walked. Taking a look at the books, he thumbed through them before shoving his hands in pockets and heaving a heavy sigh.

"Alright, so you've read them. What have you learned?" he said.

"Um— you want me to tell you everything I remember?" I asked hesitantly.

"No," he sneered. "Just a brief summary, so I know you at least retained something. Well, let's have it."

I quickly summarized what I could remember. He shifted his weight from side to side and nodded as I talked. Making sure to touch on each book I'd read, I stated all of the facts and key points I could. I was interrupted by a growl from his stomach. He glanced at the clock and frowned.

"Missed lunch again," he muttered. He held up a single finger to me and went to the office. A moment later, he returned, unwrapping a small snack bar.

"Sir?" I started.

"Huh?" he said with a mouthful.

"I came across a term while I was reading that I wasn't familiar with," I said. He raised his eyebrows, looking aggravated at why I hadn't gotten to the point yet. I continued. "What's an 'Ex'?"

"Good, you really did read. An Ex is an Ex-Royal. It's either someone who once was a Royal and for one reason or another left a Royal community, or they were found before coming to a Royal community and taken in by Ex's," he explained, plopping down on the ground against the wall. He waved at me to take a seat too.

"Why do they look down on Non-Royals?" I asked.

"Destimov was the leader of these Exes originally. He personally believed that there was no use for someone without powers to exist. He thought havin' powers made you superior. And having some particular abilities made someone even more of a superior being. He convinced some Royals of this, too. His ways were twisted. He learned that you could manipulate a power, make use of it in unimaginable ways, like torture individuals. He experimented with people and their powers. Some of these followers even died because of his methods."

"He really didn't understand or care about right and wrong, did he?" I thought aloud.

"No. He didn't. And after he was killed, someone else supposedly took lead, who also had twisted views. They likely continued with expandin' the experiments, and continued to grow in numbers. Havin' powers—abilities—can contribute to the world or tear it apart. Havin' powers and disregarding everythin' a Royal stands for, believing you are far superior, and never being satisfied with the power, is dangerous. Once your conscience is no longer somethin' you listen to, all you crave is power." Mr. Sean's voice trailed off as he played with his empty snack bar wrapper in his hands.

I sat quietly for a moment. *He doesn't seem to be talking about the textbooks anymore. This sounds like a personal experience.* The room felt larger than it did before. I didn't understand how someone could lose sight of right and wrong. It was a terrifying idea to me. I looked at Mr. Sean, who seemed lost in a memory.

"Sir," I prompted.

His expression turned sour. "Lesson's over. Tomorrow mornin' at nine, don't be late."

"Mr. —"

"Leave!" he barked. I gathered myself and left immediately, looking back at him, burying his head in his hands as I closed the door.

nine

It was nine on the dot as I entered the classroom the next morning. The room was brisker than the day before. Mr. Sean was stacking a pile of books beside the podium as I entered. He wore the same attire as yesterday. The shelves nearby seemed in a disarray.

"You're late!" he scoffed.

"I—" I stuttered, feeling flustered. "You said nine, sir."

"Just get over here," he said.

I hurried to the podium, taking a big breath. Mr. Sean's back remained to me. He stayed quiet, analyzing the stack of books now at his feet. I waited for his instruction, not daring to even breathe too loud.

"Yesterday, you learned some of the history you need to know. Today, we will move forward with your abilities, your power," he said. I took my place behind the podium. "The Sight Power can be a dangerous power to have, especially when you don't know how to control it. This ability is one of the strongest, most powerful abilities a Royal can have. There is far greater potential than most other abilities. You will need to learn your ability, how it works, what makes it tick, its limits. This can be tricky for Sights."

I felt scared of my own power. "Sir?"

He ignored me and continued. "From what Agathin told me, I think your power deals with seein' things at a distance. Do you have any control over it?"

I hung my head. "No."

"Tell me what happened outside of Banshui. Agathin said somethin' about a ball and a kid?" Mr. Sean inquired.

"Well, I saw a young boy kick a rubber ball too hard, and it was headed for Corbin. So, I stopped it.

I guess the boy was far away, maybe by some trees. I don't know." It felt silly saying it out loud. "It all happened so fast."

"Interesting," he grumbled, slowly pacing the brick flooring. "It might have to do with— or maybe—it's possible— best to just start at that though—safer—"

I shifted my weight as I watched him have the debate with himself. He sifted through the books he had in the stack. Once he was satisfied with his selection, he dropped it on the podium. I stepped to the side, allowing him room to search the book's pages for the correct chapter. Finally, he stepped aside and shoved a hand in his wrinkled trench coat pocket.

"Work on that chapter. Read through it. The next chapter, too. Work on the exercises. You will work on these until you get somewhere with them, no matter how many days it may take. Don't bother me until you've gotten somewhere," he said, pinching his brow. "Watch your clock, lunch is at noon."

Mr. Sean made his way to his office, leaving the door cracked. I stepped up to the podium and began reading. The book described how to safely activate your ability. It all sounded so foreign, but I was eager to try. A diagram showed the basics of an exercise to try for "Beginner Distance Sights."

"First, understand your space around you. Take in how open or closed the space is," I read aloud. "Take a moment to close your eyes and center yourself. Feel the floor under your feet. Take a deep breath in and let go of tension. When you open your eyes, focus on your sight alone. Let go of the feeling the rest of yourself has in the space. Stare a few feet in front of you at the ground. Take in every detail of that space. Now take an object, a book if possible, and place it at a distance from where you will be standing. If using a book, open to a random page before placing it. Repeat the exercise, trying to see every detail of the object you chose."

I reread the instructions at least three whole times before attempting any of it. As I went through each step, I found myself feeling more and more awkward. I looked at the ground in front of me and tried to focus on the details. It was fairly dusty from our shoes. I decided to move on to an object. *It suggested a book. At least you can find plenty of those around, Es.* I chose a small book from the stack by me at the podium. Opening to a page at random, I placed the book on the ground and returned to the platform by the podium.

The next couple of hours consisted of me trying the exercise over and over, to no avail. No matter how hard I tried, I couldn't tell a single detail of the book, aside from what I could normally see, that is. I couldn't read any words on the page. I couldn't tell how many paragraphs were on the page. I didn't know what the font of the text was. Nothing. I felt completely defeated. Glancing at the clock, I sighed. It was just before noon, and I had gotten nowhere.

"Sir, I'm heading to lunch!" I called. There was no answer.

I met Jewel at the door, and we headed in together to grab some food. The room was busier today than yesterday, with lots of students and teachers. Most of the teachers didn't stay in the cafeteria to eat. As we found our table and began to eat, Jewel tapped my arm.

"See that woman over there?" she said, nodding towards a kind-looking woman with her graying hair up in a bun on top of her head. "That's my teacher, Ms. Olive. She gave me a compliment today, you know. She said I was 'progressing wonderfully.' Which I guess I am. I was able to carry an entire pitcher worth of liquid today during my evaluation. What about you? How's class today?"

I looked at her as she tore off a piece of roll and stuffed it in her mouth. "It's a bit overwhelming still, but I'm getting there," I said, though I wasn't sure if the comment was supposed to comfort her, or convince myself.

"Oh, well, that's good. It may take a bit to get used to, but I'm sure you will get the hang of how everything works soon. Don't force yourself, you have only been around here for a couple days after all!" she said hopefully.

That was true. Maybe I was trying to force it too soon. I wasn't quite succeeding yet, but it was only my first day of trying. I was bound to get it right with a bit more practice. I took my orange from my plate and punctured the soft peel with my fingernail, accidentally spraying juice at the person just passing our table.

"Oh, gosh, sorry—" I stammered, looking up to see none other than Belleza glaring back at me.

"Watch it, dirt head!" she sneered.

"I didn't mean to," I said, feeling irritated.

"You really should—" she started.

"Oh, fly off, Belleza," Jewel interrupted. Belleza shot her a sour look, then rolled her eyes. She wiped the juice from her arm and marched away.

"What's with her?" I said, shaking my head.

"Oh, she's just upset because the teacher praised me in evaluations and not her. She's extra snobby when someone other than herself gets recognized. Which is ridiculous," Jewel explained. "You ready to go? I don't want to be in the way of her highness's rampage."

We cleaned up our dishes and parted ways. When I got back to the classroom, I wanted to get right back to work. Mr. Sean came out of the office with a half-eaten snack bar sticking out of his mouth and a stack of books cradled in his arms. *Did he miss lunch again today?* He didn't look at me at all, just shuffled around returning the books to the bookcases, and then disappeared into his office again.

I worked on the exercise and read the chapter of the same book over and over all afternoon. It wasn't getting me anywhere. I tried with different books as my focus. I tried standing in different areas. I even tried cupping my hands around my eyes to block my peripherals. I just wasn't getting it. It was late afternoon when I saw Mr. Sean again.

"It's three. Class is over. Go home," he said, stepping out of the office for only a moment. Before I could say anything, he had disappeared and closed the door.

———

The next couple of days went exactly the same. I woke up and arrived at nine. I worked on the same chapter, of the same book, and got the same amount of nowhere. I would have lunch, come back to find Mr. Sean hadn't had more than a snack bar for sustenance, then work on the exercise again until it was time to leave. By day four, I was getting agitated at the lack of progress I was making.

"I just don't know what I'm doing wrong," I said, picking at the remainder of my fruit on my lunch plate.

"Well, how did you do it before?" Jewel asked.

"I don't know. I never really made it happen out of choice. It just sort of, I don't know, sort of happened on its own. I don't know how to control it. I just don't know anything!" I huffed.

"Well, what are you doing different here that isn't how you made your sight happen before? Were you looking somewhere else? Were you wearing something in particular?" she brainstormed.

"Wearing something? I don't think that would have anything to do with being able to use Distance Sight." I chuckled.

"Hey! I don't know!" she shrugged. "I'm just trying to help! It's different from mine. I don't exactly know how to turn my power on or off. It just is always working."

"Yeah, I know you are trying to help." I smiled with a sigh. I thought for a moment. *What was different, Es?* "I forgot to get a juice. Did you want one?"

"No, thanks, I'm good," Jewel said, pointing to an almost full water bottle.

"I'll be right back," I said, standing.

I meandered over and grabbed for a cold juice on the counter. *Jewel is right. There's got to be something I was doing different, but what?* I was so deep in thought, I accidentally bumped right into Kasius, falling straight to the ground, and knocking the juice bottle off the counter. He pulled a hand from his pocket, and, in one quick swoop, he snatched the juice bottle just before it hit me in the face. He handed it to me, nodded, and was on his way without a word.

"Talk about reflexes," I whispered to myself, watching him stride away from me.

I gathered myself and pressed my palm against the floor to stand up. My mind went blank. I saw a figure, Kasius, passing by a table. A plate was teetering on the edge. He twitched a single finger, and the plate slid securely back onto the table. Suddenly, my surroundings returned to me. I looked around and saw the back of Kasius as he slipped out the door on the far side of the cafeteria. Jewel was in front of me, holding out a hand to help me up.

"You okay, Esmari?" Jewel asked. "You kind of zoned out for a second there. You were just staring straight ahead."

"Was I?" I asked. "Did you see that? What Kasius did?"

"No, he was over — wait!" Her face lit up. "Did you see him do something? What did he do? No, never mind that! I don't care what he did. What did you do different? You used your Sight ability somehow, didn't you?"

"Yeah, I think I did. But, how did I?" I thought for a moment as we made our way over to our table again. *I fell and* — "That's gotta be it. I was on the ground. Each time its ever happened, I wasn't actually standing up. I was kneeling or sitting or something. Either way, I was close to the ground. Do you think that could make a difference?"

"I mean, I don't really know. But it's a start!" Jewel smiled enthusiastically. "Have you tried doing that in the classroom?"

"No, not yet!" I exclaimed. "I've got to go! Thanks, Jewel!"

I gathered my plate, tucking the undrunk juice under my arm. I was eager to go back. I snatched my apple that I had saved for Mr. Sean and headed back to class. The door was closed to his office, but I placed the juice and apple next to the door for him anyway and got right to work. He peaked out of the office a few moments later and saw what I had left him. I pretended not to notice as he collected them and retreated back into the office, leaving the door cracked. Again, I opened a random book, a hand-written journal this time, and placed it on the floor. I collected myself, but this time I sat on the floor as I followed the steps instructed in the book. Still, nothing happened, though.

"This has to be it, though," I sighed.

I didn't understand. Thinking back, I went over the times I had somehow used my power. I came to the same conclusion as before. Each time, I was on the ground. *But why isn't it working now?* I felt a growing irritation boiling in my gut. My wings twitched on my back, gently brushing against the grout of the brick floor. I remembered how Jewel said her power was "always on" and sighed. Mine wasn't. It was always like a switch. It would happen when it wanted to. *You are acting like it's a person with a mind of its own, Es.*

Laughing at the thought, I adjusted myself on the hard floor and tried again. Nothing. *Okay, I won't give up now. There's got to be something I'm missing.* I pinned the book against the floor with my hand and read through the steps again. I concentrated on each step and focused on the journal across the room, trying to ignore everything else. All the sounds, all the smells; I zoned in on the journal, trying my best to block out the rest. I took a deep breath, relaxing my weight onto my hand holding open the book, and suddenly, everything went blank, except the journal. I could see it sitting on the brick. I could see each of the fibers on the textured paper. I could see how the slight breeze in the room made the spare dust particles sway on the edges of the page. I could read the inkblots and the beautiful scripted lettering at the top. *The types of Sight powers: Distance Sight, Micro Sight, Min—* Everything faded away. There was a humming in my ears. I felt hot and cold all at once.

"Esmari," a raspy voice said. "Come on, wake up."

Mr. Sean? I furrowed my eyebrow and opened my eyes slowly. The brick flooring was cold against my cheek. I blinked groggily as I got my bearings. Mr. Sean was crouched next to me. He helped me sit up from where I was laying on the ground.

"What— what happened?" I mumbled, my head still feeling foggy.

"Progress," he stated plainly. "That's enough for today. Go home. No class tomorrow."

I went back to my dorm, feeling like I could sleep for days. My whole body was exhausted and sore. I entered the room and found my messages light blinking on my phone. I pressed play and kicked off my shoes.

"Hey, Es! Call me!" Chimed Hunter's voice. I sighed with a soft smile at the familiar sound. He seemed chipper as ever. I dialed his number and slouched onto my bed.

"Hello?" a deep voice said. *Must be his roommate.*

"Uh, hi. I'm calling for Hunter. My name's Esmari."

"Ah, okay, hang on," he said. There was a clank and some muffled conversation.

"Hey Es!" Hunter said into the phone. "Haven't seen you in days! How's class going?"

I rubbed my eyes. "It's going," I said through a yawn.

"You sound exhausted. Everything okay?"

"Yeah, yeah, everything's good. Just really tired from lessons today."

"Do you want to grab a coffee later? Or, tomorrow. I have the morning free. I got loads I want to talk about," Hunter offered.

"Actually, I'm free tomorrow, too. Let's meet at The Dripping Crown at, say, nine-ish?"

We said our goodbyes, and I flopped over on my bed. A feeling of disbelief washed over me. Just a couple of weeks ago, I was wishing to be normal. To get my wings. And now, looking where I was, I got my wings, and yet, I'm still not normal. *Jokes on you, Es.* I buried my face in my pillow and groaned. I had finally gotten somewhere with my Sight. But it still didn't feel like I had a decent grasp on anything at all, especially my Sight. I suddenly missed my old bed. I missed my mom's cooking. I missed the simplicity of everything. And I just really, really wanted some peanut butter.

———

Early the next morning, I woke up to the last bit of orange glow from the sunrise filling my room. I was groggy and stiff. My stomach growled, making me realize that I never ended up eating dinner the night before. I got out of bed and went to the closet to change into a new outfit for the day. It felt nice to finally have gotten some clothing that was more my style and fit me a bit better. I brushed through my tangled hair and twisted it up into a bun, then sat at my desk. Taking out a piece of paper, I decided to write to my family. Surely Mom must be wondering how I'm settling in. Just before nine, I folded up the letter and addressed it accordingly on the back.

Ina of Athra.
From, Esmari.

Heading downstairs, I dropped it in the letter drop box to be picked up later that day. I smiled to myself thinking of Mom's face, how happy she would look when she got the letter from me. Making my way to the door, I reached out just as it swung away from me. I looked up with surprise to see Kasius peering back at me. He stepped back and held the door for me to pass. I smiled sheepishly at him. *What would Belleza think of you being so gentlemanly to me?* He nodded a silent hello, and closed the door behind him as he entered the building.

"Was Kasius just holding the door for you?" Jewel teased as she joined me.

"Yeah, so?" I blew off.

"He was looking at you. I mean, really looking at you. That's unusual for him," Jewel stated as she pondered about the encounter.

I laughed. "Hey, you have classes today? Hunter and I are grabbing coffee if you want to join."

"Lucky me! I don't have class until late this afternoon, and it's just an open lab day again. Come to think of it, we have been having a lot of those. Anyway, sounds like fun, I'll join you," she rambled.

We flew to The Dripping Crown. It was busier this morning than it was the other day when we came. Victor was hustling away at filling orders behind the counter. He caught sight of the two of us as we entered and smiled a wide grin of a greeting. I looked around, but didn't see Hunter. *Must not be here yet.* Jewel and I ordered and went upstairs to the loft area to wait for our drinks.

"So, I gotta ask," Jewel said as we settled down.

"What?" I inquired.

"What's really the deal with you and Hunter? I mean, you say he's your best friend, but, is that all? I mean he came all the way here with you." Jewel said, raising her eyebrows.

"We are just friends. Really. He's been my best friend for forever. There's nothing more there. No extra feelings. Not what you are thinking," I said.

"Yeah, I know *you* say that. But, does he know. I mean, I see the way you two interact. And he's so attentive and sweet to you!" she continued.

"No way. The friendship thing is mutual. No feelings on either end." I couldn't help but chuckle thinking about us being together as a couple.

Hunter clomped up the stairs seeming out of breath. "Hey!"

"Speaking of—" Jewel said. I rolled my eyes.

"You two were talking about me? Were you talking about my good looks?" he joked, standing up tall with his nose in the air and smoothing back his hair dramatically.

"No, we were talking about how you ate a bug, thinking it would make your wings grow faster," I teased.

"Once! I only did that once! When I was four! And your brother is the one who told me to!" he defended.

"Yeah, you did believe anything he said back then," I winced with a chuckle at the memory.

Jewel giggled. "That's funny. And I can't believe you actually ate a bug," she said, scrunching her nose up in disgust at the thought.

"Moving on," Hunter frowned. "I'm actually glad that both of you girls are here, I need some advice! Some, you know, girl advice."

I looked at Jewel and shrugged smugly. "I think that answers your question." I turned back to Hunter just as Victor was joining us with our drinks. "Alright, who's the girl?"

"Oh, I joined at the right time," Victor smiled.

"Okay, her name is Flow. And she's super nice. I toured some courses and found that I really liked the carpentry class. Not just liked the class, but I'm actually good at it. I mean, I haven't tried it a whole ton—" He paused and looked at Jewel, who was struggling to understand the direction of his story. "Right, right, uh, getting to the point. So, anyway, I joined the basics course of carpentry and in walks this girl. She's really pretty, and she's talented, too. She's kind of quiet and seems shy. I don't think she even knows I exist." Hunter gushed.

"Well, have you talked with her?" I asked.

"No."

"Introduced yourself?" Jewel chimed.

"No."

"Have you even said hello to her?" I asked.

"No." Hunter sighed.

"Welp, there's your first step." I smiled, waving my hands in front of me.

"She's right. The scariest part about talking to girls is getting the courage to strike up the conversation. From there, the conversation will either flow, or it won't," shrugged Victor. The bell on the door jingled as another customer came in. "And, that's my cue." He excused himself and headed downstairs.

"Yeah, okay, I guess I'll try," Hunter said, lost in thought.

"So," Jewel said. "Carpentry, huh?"

"Yeah!" Hunter perked right back up. "I'm only in the beginning course, but I'm really into it. And one of the masters was there yesterday, and he said I've got some real potential. I guess he owns some sort of shop over in West District. His name was something with an 'H' I think. Hector? No, no. That's not it—"

"Hank?" Jewel said.

"Yeah! I think that was his name! How'd you know?" Hunter said.

She took a sip of her coffee. "He's my uncle. It's actually quite the compliment to be recognized by him. He's very good at what he does."

Hunter's eyes widened, and he grinned that great big goofy grin of his. "Really?"

"Yeah, really. He likes to go to those classes and keep an eye on people as possible apprentices," Jewel explained.

"No way! I could be an apprentice. Es, can you imagine it? Me as a carpenter's apprentice! And I could build— stuff— or, or— carve stuff for you guys. Of course, I should probably find my knack. But maybe I'll be a master violin carver, or make the perfect chair!" Hunter rambled. "I mean, the possibilities are endless!"

Jewel grabbed some of the condensation off of her cup and began playing with it in her hand. It seemed like a natural thing she did out of habit. I was still getting used to it. Hunter's jaw dropped, and he stared in awe at it. Jewel caught his look and chuckled, looking at her hand.

"I forget that you two aren't used to seeing

this," Jewel said.

"Is that your power?" Hunter asked.

"Yup, in all its glory," Jewel said sarcastically. "It's kind of fun sometimes, though it makes something like washing your hands or taking a shower a bit more of a task."

"Hey, speaking of powers, how's your class going? How's your teacher and stuff?" Hunter asked me suddenly.

I groaned. "It took me all week to just do one task. And supposedly, I did it, but I don't feel like I really did it right. I still don't have any control or any idea how to control my sight. I don't know."

"I know you'll get the hang of it, Es," Hunter reassured.

"It's just, I'm in this room that's just me and books. All I do is read and try to follow the instructions in the book, while my teacher hides away in his office working on—on—well, who knows what! He doesn't seem to like me, or anything, or anyone." I huffed.

"Esmari, don't be too hard on yourself. This is all new to you. Most of us Royals were brought up around other Royals. We were taught about abilities early on, and when we got our wings and abilities, we were prepared because we had usually seen a parent or a friend with a power." Jewel smiled. "Plus, you said you got somewhere this week, you used your power? Right?"

"Yeah, I suppose," I sighed, drinking the last gulp of my coffee.

Victor came most of the way up the stairs, hanging off the side railing. "Hey, Jewels, wanna make some extra cash? It's getting pretty busy, and I could use a hand?"

"Sure!" she said excitedly. She gathered her cup and followed Victor downstairs.

Hunter and I chatted more about his interest in carpentry and what he was learning in the class. He really seemed to light up when he talked about it, which made me happy to see. *I'm really glad he's fitting in here.* He talked about the dorm he was sharing and how the other Non-Royals were treating him.

"Ah, man!" Hunter exclaimed, looking at the little clock hanging on the wall. It was nearly noon. "I gotta get going. You really should come by my dorm sometime and meet my roommate and some of the others. They're really cool."

"Yeah? That sounds like fun! Let me know when!" I smiled back.

Hunter gathered his things and was on his way. I sat for a moment longer, listening to the chatter downstairs. Everyone seemed to be in an upbeat spirit. They all had a purpose about their ways. Jewel looked so happy as she hustled away, making the drink orders. She would listen for Victor's instructions and learned along the way. Every drink she made right, her smile would grow, and so would her customer's smile. I watched as she took the water from the faucet in her hand and tossed it into a cup that Victor held out to her. He cheered. They laughed. She fit here. I envied her bliss.

I wonder what that feels like? What it's like to understand your power? I pondered to myself. I watched my friend a moment longer, enjoying the pure joy that radiated from her. Finally, I decided I had sat there long enough. I gathered my cup and headed downstairs, setting my dirty cup on the counter for Victor before turning to the door.

"Hold up!" Victor called, grabbing a small to-go box and holding it out to me. "I've got an extra sandwich here, want it? No charge."

"Free? What's the catch?" I joked, eyeing him dramatically.

"Ha. Ha," he mocked. "No catch. Here, take it."

"Thanks," I said with a smile, "Bye, you two!"

"Bye!" Jewel called over her shoulder as she steamed some milk.

I headed out the door and paused, not really knowing where I was headed. I didn't want to go back to my dorm, and I didn't have class today, either. Since Hunter and Jewel were busy, I was left on my own. *I guess I have the rest of the day to myself.* I took a deep breath in, and a salty breeze from the shoreline touched my nose. Before I knew it, I was flying myself to the beach.

It was beautiful. Like nothing I had ever seen. The sunlight danced on the water as the white foam from the waves licked the sand. A mother and small child were building a sandcastle nearby. I watched as the child stacked the sand higher and higher, then looked slyly at the mother. He wound back and pushed both arms into the side of the mound, sending the entire thing tumbling apart. The mother laughed. A couple walked along the tideline, shoes in hand, letting the water lap up against their toes. I took off my sandals and held them with the crooks of my fingers.

Gently, I took my first step in the velvety beach sand. It was such an odd feeling as it shifted below the pads of my feet. I walked toward the water watching the sand stick to my feet like static. A breeze brushed by me again, tossing some stray strands of hair out of my face. The sound of the waves was so soothing to my ears. I took a breath in and dipped a toe in a nearby wave just as it began to retreat from where I was. It was cool compared to the warm sand. I stepped onto the muddy spot left behind by the last wave and waited for the next to come crashing in, wetting my feet up to my ankles. I giggled like a little kid. Staying right where I was, I opened the sandwich box and began to eat. I watched as each time a wave came and went, it buried my feet deeper in the mud.

My mind went back to class; back to the breakdown of how to activate my power. I went over the steps in my mind. I thought over yesterday, how I used my Sight. I wanted so badly to be able to control my ability. *It just happens when it wants to, not when I try to.* I frowned, closing my now empty box. I looked out on the horizon for a moment and decided to try to use my Sight again. Carefully, I went through each step one by one, but nothing happened. I wasn't sure if I was disappointed, though. I wasn't even surprised in the least. *It was worth a try, Es.*

A familiar cackle made me cringe. Belleza. She and Lilly were just a short distance away, wading in the water with a couple of their other friends. I debated for a moment whether I wanted to even stick around. *No, there's no reason I need to leave, just because she's here.* I made up my mind and gave myself a reassuring nod. As I freed my feet from the depths of the squishy mud, I glanced over at Belleza and Lilly once more. Belleza was moving the water back and forth with ease, performing for her friend. Lilly applauded as she brought a ball of water up into the air without touching it, then with a swoop, she tossed it as far as she could back into the ocean. I hated to admit it, but it was interesting to see.

I found a nearby trash can and tossed in my now empty to-go box. Walking back over near the water, I plopped down in some dry sand. I set my sandals beside me and ran my hands through the soft grains of the beach sand. I closed my eyes and blocked out all the sounds except the ocean. It was relaxing and peaceful. I took a deep breath of the salty air, enjoying the moment.

Before I knew it, the afternoon was welcoming the evening. I brushed off and headed for my dorm. Pausing, I took one last look. The crash of the waves on the beach brought a smile to my lips. *Mom would like it here.* I flittered up into the sky to fly back.

When I arrived at the dorm, it was particularly quiet. I could hear the rustling of the wind in the trees. I went up the stairs in my building and passed through the seating area heading for my dorm. A sound of a page being turned caught my attention. I could see the outline of Kasius's head bowed as he scribbled in a notebook while sitting in a nearby chair. I passed by him quietly. *I don't think he even noticed me.*

I arrived at my door and entered, tossing my shoes off and heading for the shower. Taking a look in the mirror, I noticed a pinker tone to my skin. *Great, sunburnt.* Thankfully, not too bad. I showered and put on some comfy clothes for the night. A light tap on the door surprised me as I towel dried my hair.

"Just a second!" I called, tossing the towel down and hurrying to the door.

I straightened my shirt and opened the door. There was no one there, just a small jar and a note. I stepped out and looked around. No one was in the hall. Kasius was still in the same spot as before, still working away at the notebook. *Huh, that's weird.* I took the items into the room and shut the door.

"Use this on that sunburn of yours. It'll be gone by tomorrow," I read aloud. There was no signature.

When I opened the jar, I was pleased to take a whiff of its familiar scent. Aloe lotion with a little hint of lavender, just like my mom used to make for Bray and me. I slathered the lotion on my sunburn and relaxed to the cooling sensation as it soaked in. There was still quite a bit left in the small jar, which I put under my sink in the bathroom. As I crawled into bed, a thought wouldn't leave my mind.

"I wonder who left that for me?" I said to myself.

ten

A couple of weeks went by, and I was making very little progress on my Sight. Mr. Sean had started to warm up to me, however. Every day, he at least would greet me in person, which was a step. He also seemed to scowl at me a little less. But he was still really bad at remembering to eat, getting so caught up in whatever it was that he was doing in his office. I would be sure to bring him a little something to eat each day after lunch. He never said, but I think he was secretly grateful to not live off of snack bars.

This morning, I came in to find him waiting for me by the podium with a new book in hand. He seemed particularly calm, and if I'm not mistaken, I may have almost seen a glimmer of happiness in his eye when he saw me. The operative word being *almost*. He shoved one hand in his pocket of the same old trench coat he always seemed to be wearing and waved me over with the other hand.

"You have been makin' some progress on the exercises you've been workin' on. Very slow progress, but progress. We at least know that you are for sure a Sight," Mr. Sean said. I couldn't tell if the tone of his voice was proud or disgusted. "I figured we should switch it up and try somethin' else. And by we, I mean you. Work through this chapter I have open for you."

"Yes, sir," I said.

He turned on his heel and headed to his office. "Watch your time," he reminded as always.

The book was explaining how to walk through a room with your mind. Taking note of little details that you see. It was a very interesting concept, and I was eager to try. At the bottom of the page, listing all the steps, there was a scribbled note.

Only works in open room.

"Open room? Meaning what?" I thought aloud. "I wonder if it means only the room that I'm in?"

I shrugged it off and began going through the steps one by one. Over and over, I attempted, but got nowhere. Finally, I sat on the ground and tried one last time, only to be disappointed again. I grunted with frustration. This seemed to be a constant occurrence of not succeeding. For once, I wanted it to just work! I slammed my hands against the wood flooring of the platform.

The sounds of the room grew quiet. My mind went blank. I could see across the room in the very back corner, was a stack of books. Three of them, all neat in a stack on the ground and —

And then the sound of the room came rushing back into my ears. *I did it! Well, something anyway.* It wasn't like what the book talked about. It didn't feel like I was taking steps, but I could see something that was across the room. A detail. *But, how?* I walked through what had just happened in my mind. I was already on the ground. *Maybe, it didn't have to do with being on the ground.* I looked at my hands for a moment and thought back. *Do I have to touch the ground to make it happen?*

A growl in my stomach shook me out of my

thoughts. I glanced at the clock. Almost twelve-thirty! I was running late! I hurried out of the room and to the cafeteria, where it was already fairly barren. I went to the counter to order some food. Decided on a chicken and rice bowl, and an apple for Mr. Sean. Then slid down to grab a juice. *Out of mango, just your luck for being late, Es.* I sighed and reached for a water.

"Hey, wait. You're Esmari, right?" said Ben, the person who usually made my food.

"Yeah?' I responded.

"Here, I was told to save this for you," he said, handing me a bottle of juice.

Mango. "But—who—" I stuttered. He just shrugged and smiled.

I turned with my lunch in hand and glanced around for Jewel. She had her head ducked down, slurping the last of her soup. I joined her and smiled as she wiped the tomato soup mustache off her top lip with a napkin.

"Hey!" I greeted. "Did you, by chance, ask them to save me a juice at the counter?"

"Nope, why?" she said. I shrugged at her, and she glanced at the clock. "I hate to bail on you, but I have got to get back to class. Today is the last day for our big project we have been working on, and I am so far from being done."

"Aw, but I just got here!" I wined. "Alright,

go."

"After classes, my dorm, snacks, music, girl chat. I'm not taking no for an answer. I'll see you then!" She rushed out of the room.

I sat and ate my lunch, still pondering about the mystery person who saved the drink for me. *If it wasn't Jewel, then who was it? And how did they know I liked the mango one?* I frowned at myself for being so predictable. When I had finished, I headed back to the class with the apple in hand for Mr. Sean. I entered the classroom, and to my surprise, Mr. Sean was not in his office, for once. He looked over, and I tossed the apple in his direction. He caught it without a problem.

"So," he said, shining the apple on his shirt. "Have you gotten anywhere?"

"With the lesson, you mean? Yeah, I think so," I said. A part of me felt that I shouldn't tell him about my needing to touch the ground. At least not yet.

"Great. I have placed a ball on one of the bookshelves in the room. Find it. Tell me what color it is," he said, plopping down against the wall and biting into his apple. He closed his eyes and leaned his head back.

"Uh, okay," I said, feeling very unsure of myself. I sat on the ground and took a deep breath.

Mr. Sean's eyes opened, and he went to take

another bite. Hesitating, he looked at me, confused. "Why are you on the ground?"

"It's the only way I've been able to—" I tried to explain.

He shrugged, closing his eyes again. "Whatever," he mumbled through a mouthful of apple.

Okay, Esmari. Let's try this. I placed my hands beside me on the ground concentrating on finding the ball. The room was silent, aside from Mr. Sean smacking away at the apple. It was distracting. *Ignore it, Es, find the ball.* The more I tried, the less I felt like I was getting anywhere. *Who was I kidding? I had never been able to control it before, why did I think I could now?* I sat there, attempting for over an hour. Finally, I was exhausted and frustrated. *I thought I was really on to something this time.*

"Come take a break. You are trying to force it," Mr. Sean said. It was the most sincere I had ever heard him be.

I joined him, sitting on the edge of the platform. "Mr. Sean, how does your Sight work? Are you a Distance Sight, too?"

"Wondered when you were going to ask about that." He paused and took a great big sigh. "Yeah, I'm sort of a Distance Sight. The thing about Sights, well powers really, is they are different person to person. Sometimes, you might have a power like someone else, but not exactly. Or you might be exactly like someone else. Anyway, I can see everythin' in the room or space around me. My Sight, as with most Sights, stops at a closed door."

"Only works in open room," I remembered.

"Yeah, pretty much. I can see around objects in a room or around the corner of a hallway. And I see all of it all the time. There's no turnin' it off for me. It just always is workin'. Every detail, every item, every person. All. The. Time. Within a specific distance, that is. In larger spaces, I sometimes have to try to see to the other side of the room. And it's not like I can see the whole city, thankfully." He explained. He paused for a moment and pinched his brow. I found myself genuinely surprised at how openly he talked about his Sight with me.

"Does it hurt?" I asked. I felt bad for him.

"Yeah. Gives me a headache sometimes. Strains my eyes," he said bluntly. "Okay, that's enough. Go get the book on the bottom shelf there, third from the right. Blue cover."

I did as he said. "This one?" I asked, holding it out to him. It was the journal I was using for my exercise a few weeks back.

"Yup," he said, thumbing through it. He handed it back to me open. "Read through this since you are so curious about Sight powers."

"Sure." I nodded.

He stood to his feet with a grunt and began walking to his office. "Still need to find the ball." He called over his shoulder, waving his apple core at me.

Right. I sighed. Feeling unmotivated to try again at the exercise, I slumped down on the floor and looked over the book in my hands. It was well worn. The script was beautiful, and just as I remembered the other day.

The types of Sight powers: Distance Sight, Micro Sight, Mind Sight, Visionary Sight —

"This is a long list!" I whispered to myself, skimming down to where the list ended on the bottom of the page.

I read on about the different types of Sights, mostly skimming until I came across something about a Distance Sight. I figured that was a bit more important information, seeing as I was one. *I could always go back and re-read this at another time.* After some time relaxing and learning a bit of history about Distance Sights, I decided it was time to try again at the exercise.

I set the book aside and readjusted myself on the cool brick flooring. I placed my hands purposefully in front of me and focused. Pressing firmly against the ground with my palms, I focused on the search, clearing my mind of any outside thoughts. Several attempts, and an unknown amount of time later, I finally saw it. The space around me disappeared, and, very clearly, I could see a ball. *Green.*

I jumped up with excitement. I was finally getting somewhere! Skipping over to the office, I raised a very confident hand and tapped on the door that was propped open by a wedge of wood. My face smiled with pride, and I took a satisfied sigh, glancing in the room. Mr. Sean was sitting on the ground, gathering up papers that lay around him.

"Well?" he asked.

"It's green." I grinned with pride.

"Where?" he asked.

My heart sank. My ears grew hot. "Where what?" I asked, already knowing the answer.

"The ball. Where was it?" He asked.

"Um," I gulped. I didn't know where it was. I only saw the ball. That was it.

"If you can tell me the color, then you know where it is," he stated. He looked up for a moment with an angry, almost confused expression. It wasn't exactly directed at me, I don't think. He shook his head in disagreement with his own thoughts. "Go home. You can be done for today."

It was quiet in the halls as I exited the school. The air felt different outside. Something felt off, but I couldn't quite put my finger on what it was. Part of me thought it was just the mix of emotions duking it out inside my head that made the world seem off. There wasn't anyone outside the dorm like there usually was either, though. That was something that I knew I wasn't imagining in my head. I entered my dorm building and headed upstairs, where I started to hear some chatter in the lounge seating area. A small group was gathered, and I could hear Belleza talking in her high-pitched voice.

" — It was so scary." she squeaked.

I went straight to Jewel's dorm and tapped on the open door.

"Es! Hey, come on in. Close the door behind you, will ya?" Jewel said.

I went inside and plopped down on the bean bag I had jokingly deemed to be "my spot." Jewel brought over an armful of snacks and drinks and settled down beside me.

"What's up with Belleza and her entourage?" I asked, laying back and listening to the beans in the bean bag settle below my head.

"You didn't hear?" Jewel said, surprised.

"Hear what? Did she break a fingernail or something?" I laughed.

"No, Belleza encountered an Ex over in West District today," Jewel said with a serious tone.

I sat up in shock. "She what?" I exclaimed.

"Yeah, an Ex." Jewel nodded. "I guess the guy disappeared before he was caught. But, I guess they were, like, scoping out the area or something. I can't even imagine what she did. It's a surprise they weren't savage toward her or anything. She's actually rather lucky."

We both cringed at the thought of her being *lucky*. "But seriously, they are really that dangerous, huh?" I said.

"Yeah, I mean, more so if you are a Non-Royal. But if you are in their way, I don't think they care much either way. And they manipulate their powers. They have learned dark ways to use them, almost mutate the power. They have a really twisted sense of reality." Jewel shuttered.

"What do you think you would do if you ever saw one," I asked.

"Well, I'm really hoping I don't. I wish they all disappeared. But I'd like to think I'd stand up to them. I mean, I have plenty of Non-Royals that are family and a lot of Non-Royal friends, too. And that is a big basis of being an Ex, supposedly. The whole wanting to do away with anyone who doesn't have abilities, and whatnot," Jewel said.

"Yeah. I don't like that," I agreed.

"If you had to fight one, you think you would?" Jewel asked

I thought for a moment. "If I had no other choice, I'd fight, I guess. But I doubt I'd last very long. Let's just hope that never happens."

eleven

The following day, it seemed like most students were afraid to leave their dorms. It was quieter on campus, too, I noticed as Jewel and I walked into the academy together. We parted ways at the entrance, promising to have lunch together today. I went to class, only to find a note taped to the door for me.

Esmari, work on the same thing as yesterday. Tell me

tomorrow.
-Mr. Sean
PS no cheating.

"Yes, sir," I mumbled to myself as I entered the classroom.

It almost felt odd being in the class alone. Even though Mr. Sean was always tucked away in his office, at least it was someone there. Another soul. But today, it was just me and the books. *Alright, Es, let's get right to it.* I sat in the middle of the open floor and just relaxed for a moment, allowing my hands to rest on the cool ground. I cleared my mind of everything, wanting a clean slate to start the morning on. Closing my eyes and listened to my own breath. I could feel my wings on my back, brushing the ground where I sat as the air in the room blew against them. I was safe. I could feel that. But something in me felt agitated. It was uncomfortable. I didn't understand the feeling. I opened my eyes and pushed the feeling out of my mind.

"You've got to find that green ball, Es," I said to myself.

I began trying the exercise over and over. I focused on the green ball I had seen yesterday. Yet, no matter what I did, I couldn't see anything but that in my head. None of the surroundings, no indications of where in the room it was, just the green ball. I felt like I was forcing it to work. But it was like my power had a mind of its own. I sighed and shook my head, feeling defeated.

"These exercises get me nowhere," I grunted. "Fine, what if I don't force it? What if I don't have an agenda?"

I smiled at the thought. *What if that was it?* I looked at my hands, feeling more determined. I once again cleared my mind, this time not even thinking about the ball. I didn't want to find anything. I didn't want to be led anywhere. I just wanted my power to work. Gently, I touched my fingers to the ground in front of me and waited. I sat there in a calm meditative state, just waiting and breathing.

The smallest surge went through me, something I never noticed before. My mind went blank, my surroundings faded away. I breathed. I could see the books on the podium where I had left them. The journal I was reading yesterday became so vivid. I could see each fiber on the paper.

My surroundings came back. I shook my head and pressed my lips into a smile. I felt weak momentarily, weak but proud of the progress. I glanced at the clock, which read just after twelve. Excited, I stood up and nearly skipped to the door.

I paused for a moment and looked back with a sudden feeling of conflicting emotions inside me. I had gotten somewhere, but I wasn't in control of my power at all. I didn't find the location of the ball, which was the entire task. Three hours I was sitting there, and I was only able to use my Sight once.

My stomach growled and reminded me about lunch once again. I left the room and closed the door behind me. Spinning around, I found the hallways a bit more eerie than normal the way they echoed in their emptiness. Once in the cafeteria, it was almost no different. There were very few students here, and even a teacher was having lunch in the corner of the room today. Jewel waved at me from a nearby table.

"Go grab your lunch, I saved you a seat!" she said with a smile.

I retrieved my food and drink and went to sit with her. She was happily eating away at her sandwich. She seemed a little extra chipper. It was comforting to see. I glanced around the cafeteria again. Belleza and Lilly were only a few tables away. They were quieter than normal today, so much so that I barely noticed they were there. Kasius was sitting alone at the table next to them with a book in his hand. I stared at the cover of his book for a moment. It was plain blue, all except for a couple metallic stars in one of the corners. Kasius' brow furrowed for a moment then relaxed, his eyes just visible above the top of the book.

"Um, hello? Earth to Esmari?" Jewel said, waving a hand in front of my face.

I blinked and smirked at Jewel. "What's put you in such a cheery mood?"

"Were you not listening to me at all?" she asked.

Had she been talking? "Sorry," I frowned.

"It's cool. My teacher gave us an extra couple of days for our projects. And I already finished mine, which means I get to have open lab time for the next couple of days." She smiled.

"Open what?"

"Ah, right, sorry, your class works different than most. It just means that I can work on anything I want to," she clarified.

"Oh, neat!" I said, taking a bite of fruit.

"How's your class today?" Jewel asked.

I thought for a moment. "It's good. Mr. Sean isn't there today. So, I'm just working on my lesson. Not that today is any different, I usually do whatever task he has for me on my own as it is, but I think I am finally starting to understand how my power works. At least a little."

"That's great, Es!" Jewel said approvingly. "Wait, your class is in the back of the school, right?

Isn't it a little creepy, you know, being back there on your own, especially with what happened?"

"What? You mean the Ex yesterday? I don't know, it's usually really quiet back there. The classrooms around us don't seem to be used much," I shrugged. Looking away, I noticed Kasius peering over his book at me, listening in on the conversation. His gaze held mine for a moment, before he casually looked back at his book.

"Well, okay. Just be sure not to stay too late today," Jewel said. "Oh, have you talked to Hunter yet? About all of it?"

"No, I called this morning and left a message," I sighed.

We chatted a bit more as we finished our lunch and then headed back to our classes. I entered the class feeling refreshed. Sitting back down in the middle of the floor, just as before, I felt determined to find the ball or, at the very least, use my power again. I touched the brick with my fingertips. Clearing my mind, I waited.

An hour passed, and I still remained in the same spot as before. I tried focusing my thoughts on the green ball. After another thirty minutes went by, I gave myself a rest and thumbed through the pages of the journal about Distance Sights again. I looked for an answer as to why touching the ground helped activate my power. I found nothing.

That seemed odd to me.

"Mr. Sean said that each person's power is different," I recalled. "Maybe that's just how mine happens to work."

I returned the journal to the podium, placing myself back on the floor, and got back to the exercise. I took in a breath of the musky air and focused on all of my senses. I observed how the textured brick felt against the pads of my fingers. How the cool air brushed against my cheek. How my shirt moved as I breathed. I felt my hair against my neck. And then I blocked all of those out of my mind. I let them all melt away like a distant memory. I closed my eyes, and I felt a mix of emotions and something else, something I couldn't quite identify, swirling inside my chest.

I opened my eyes once again and let my gaze fall to nowhere in particular. Again, I entered into a meditative state, not thinking of anything in particular, not listening, not aware. *Show yourself, little green ball. Show me where you are hiding.*

I don't know how long I sat there before my Sight happened. I saw the green ball so very clearly, but nothing else. I strained to see something, anything around it. I could feel my power stronger than before, but I still had no control. It was as if it were fighting me. I strained my Sight more to try to get a glimpse of its surroundings, a shadow, a reflection. It seemed like there was nothing around it for me to see. I found myself feeling the room get larger and larger. Then my Sight jumped from the ball to the open journal once again. I tried to pull away my Sight from the journal, back to the ball.

My surroundings came back around me. There was a buzzing in my ears. My arms and hands were stiff from pressing into the floor so hard, unknowingly. I shook my head and covered my ears momentarily to silence the buzzing. The room was darker than before. *How long had I sat there?* I glanced at the clock.

"Five thirty?" I gasped. My head felt woozy. *Had it really been that long?*

I stood and left the room, heading for the dorms. My mind was in a fog of confusion. The barren halls echoed as I made my way through the academy. It felt odd being here this late. Almost like I was unintentionally trespassing. I exited the academy and walked the path to the dorms. A movement in the corner of my eye caught my attention. Belleza and Lilly stepped in front of my path.

"You sure are studying late," Belleza noted.

"Yeah, I guess I got distracted," I shrugged. *I don't need to explain myself to you, Belleza.*

"I suppose you have a lot more lessons to catch

up on. I mean, you probably didn't have a good foundation to your education in that town you are from. What was the name? Al—Ath—"

"Athra."

"Right, Athra. Did they all dress like you there, too?" she said, scrunching her face and glancing over my clothing. Lilly giggled.

"Belleza, what do you what?" I asked plainly. I didn't feel like playing her games.

She raised a hand gracefully with a nasty smirk on her face. Suddenly, a tall figure stepped between us. Kasius stared down Belleza with a stone face.

"Kasius!" Belleza exclaimed with a smile.

"Knock it off," he said. It was the first time I had heard him talk. His voice was different than I would have expected. It was smooth with a slight calming nature to it.

Belleza lowered her hand and sighed dramatically. "You're no fun," she pouted.

Kasius stepped between her and Lilly, making them clear a path for him to pass. I paused for a moment, then decided to follow him. We walked for a bit, until just out of earshot of Belleza and Lilly, before he stopped in his tracks. I stopped abruptly just a few steps behind and studied his movements. He turned slightly to me, one hand in the pocket of his slacks, the other resting at his side.

His light blue button-down shirt was rolled at the sleeves and fit his chiseled features well.

"You okay?" he finally said.

"Yeah. I'm fine," I said.

He gave a soft smile and nodded, then turned away.

"I had it handled, you know," I mentioned softly.

He glanced over his shoulder. "I know," he said, then walked away like nothing ever happened. I looked down at my blue jeans and forest green blouse for a moment thinking back to what Belleza said. I shrugged and shook my head. *I think I look nice.*

"Hey! Es!" Called a voice.

I looked over to find Hunter waving at me from down the way. Walking next to him was a guy about his size. They both looked happy as they joined me.

"Hey, Es. This is Finn," Hunter introduced.

"Hi," Finn said. His voice was familiar.

"Hunter's roommate? Right?" I asked.

"Yeah, how'd you know? Did Hunter tell you about me? All terrible things I'm sure," Finn said sarcastically.

I laughed. "I recognized your voice from the phone," I said. "I'm glad to see you are okay, after what I heard yesterday."

"What? Oh, you mean the Ex. Yeah, no big." Hunter shrugged and changed the subject. "We are meeting with a couple friends. You know, some other Non-Royals. Want to come?"

"Sure!" I paused. "You think they'd be okay with me tagging along?"

"Eh, I don't think they'd have a problem with it. Come on, it would be fun to have you!" Finn said.

"Yeah, Es. Please join us!" Hunter begged, tugging at my arm. I smiled and rolled my eyes. "I'm taking that as a yes."

The two of them led me to their dorms. The buildings were a bit different than ours. Less modern in a way. We met three others in the downstairs seating area of their dorm building who happily greeted us and made room for us to join them.

"Everyone, this is Esmari. Esmari, this is Darren, Moz, and that's Flow," Hunter pointed out. I smirked at him flashing him a look. *So, this is the girl.* He nudged me.

"Hi! It's nice to meet you," I said politely.

"So, you're the Royal," Darren said.

I nodded, feeling uncomfortable.

"What's your power?" Finn asked, passing me a bottle of water.

"I'm a Sight," I said. They all exchanged looks

and nodded in approval. I didn't like the attention. "What are all of you studying? Flow, I think Hunter said that you were studying carpentry?" Hunter swallowed, nudging me again. I nudged back.

"Yeah, that's right," she smiled and looked at Hunter sheepishly.

"I'm studying herbs and medicine," chimed Finn pridefully.

"Darren and I are both studying multiple things. We haven't really found what we like yet. But I'm leaning towards something in the history field. Darren hasn't found something he's good at yet." Moz teased.

Darren chucked a pillow at him. "Hey! I am good at flying!" he defended.

"Actually, you're even bad at that!" Finn smiled. The group laughed.

"Not true!" Darren said, standing to his feet. "I'm faster than you."

"Race! Race! Race!" Moz chanted. Hunter joined in. "Race! Race!"

"You're on!" Finn smiled, eagerly accepting the challenge.

We all exited the dorm and found a decent starting spot. The two guys shook hands and began to hover above the ground. They exchanged some small banter and got themselves ready.

"Okay, first one around the dorm buildings wins!" Moz said. "On your marks, get set, go!"

And off they went. We cheered for them both and clapped our hands. I tried to keep an eye on the two as they disappeared around the first corner. We all looked in the other direction watching for them to come in to the finish. The air was cool and smelled of the wildflowers and grass at our feet. The golden glow of the sunset was beautiful as it reflected against the windows of the nearby dorm buildings. I felt elated and at peace all at once. Hunter's gaze fell on Flow, standing just in front of him. I smiled to myself. I had never seen him like this. So happy.

Darren came bursting past the finish line with Finn closely behind. They both landed to the ground with big grins on their faces. The two gave each other a high five, panting and laughing.

Darren threw his arms up. "Yes!" he exclaimed. "Okay, who's next? Who wants to lose to the great Darren flyer!"

"I nominate Es!" Hunter said with a wide grin.

"Hunter! No—" I said, backing away.

"Come on, Royal. Am I not a formidable opponent for you?" Darren lured.

Moz nudged at my back. "Come on, Esmari! Let's see you fly."

I gritted my teeth. "Fine."

"You are so going down, Darren!" Hunter taunted.

Finn stepped up to us as we began to hover above the ground. "Okay, rules. No powers, Esmari. We gotta keep it fair." I nodded. "Follow the outside of the buildings. It will make a loop back here. You can't get lost. First one around wins. Ready—"

I closed my eyes and took a breath.

"Set—"

Opening my eyes, I ignored the sounds around me and focused on the buildings in the dimming light.

"GO!"

Off we raced. The adrenaline kicked in like a rush all throughout my body. I smiled from excitement. I had forgotten what it felt like to fly as fast as my wings would take me. Faster and faster I went, the wind rushing through the strands of my hair. I rounded the first building and hardly looked around to see my surroundings. I couldn't hear the sound of Darren's wings anymore beside me. Each time I turned, I zoned in on my next corner until I rounded the last one. I could see Hunter's smiling face at the finish line. I got an extra surge of energy and gave it everything I had, blasting past the finish line. A few moments later, Darren finished and crumpled into a heap on the ground.

Still panting, I went over to Darren. "You good?" I laughed.

He lifted a hand and patted the ground. "I admit defeat. You win. You win," he huffed.

"Yes! Go, Es!" Hunter cheered.

I flopped on the ground next to Darren and looked up into the sky just as the first stars were peeking out. The others joined us. I was exhausted, but happy. It was the first time in a while I had really let go and had some fun. I loved the feeling I had when I was racing. I smiled to myself and thought of Bray. The way he would come in glistening with sweat after racing with his friends all morning. He would always look so happy and carefree after a wing race.

"What's up, Es?" Hunter said, throwing an arm on my shoulder.

"I just finally realized why Bray was racing all the time," I said, playing with my necklace between my fingertips. "It makes you feel free."

twelve

Two weeks had gone by, and I found that carefree feeling faded away faster than I wanted it to. I re-read the letters I had gotten from home and felt a pit in my stomach growing. Taking a big sigh, I folded the letters back up and stashed them away in the desk drawer. A rapid knock on my door startled me.

"Come in!" I called.

Jewel burst through the door. "You need to call

Hunter."

"What's going on?" I asked, my voice wavering.

"The Ex's have left a threat on the carpentry building. Es, they were there. Somebody threatened the Non-Royals," Jewel said.

My heart pounded in my chest. "When? Did they catch who it was?"

"No, supposedly, no one was there at the time. It was burnt onto the roof, the guy wasn't caught, I don't think," Jewel explained.

I grabbed the phone and dialed Hunter's number.

"Hello?" Finn's voice said on the other end.

"Hi, it's Es."

"Oh, hang on, I'll put you on speaker." There was a pause and a beep from the button. "Es? You there?"

"Yeah, still here."

"Hey Es! Am I glad to hear you! Hey, Corbin's here too."

"Hello, Esmari," Corbin said with a somber voice.

"Are you guys all okay? Jewel just told me what happened."

"Yeah, we're okay. No, one was there at the time. Flow is a bit shook up. She's the one who found the message," Hunter explained.

"What are they saying?" Jewel beckoned, tugging at my sleeve.

"Oh, hang on, let me put it on speaker— there— Jewel is here with me on speaker," I said.

"Hey," Jewels greeted.

"So, what did it say?" I asked.

"They warned us to watch our backs," Finn stated. It was quiet.

"Well, I'm just glad no one got hurt," I said finally.

"We get a mini vacation out of it, though. They are shutting down classes for a couple of days while this is investigated and cleaned up. They don't want us going into a burning building, being that it's filled with wood and all," Hunter said, trying to lighten the mood.

"You really are a goofball," Finn chuckled.

"Hey, Es, we gotta go," Corbin said. "But, Maya should be around your area this morning to check in with you."

We said our goodbyes and hung up. I brushed through my hair, and Jewel and I sat in silence for a moment, reflecting on it all. After a little while, she and I both headed downstairs to make our way to the academy for the day. We met Maya just outside.

"Esmari," Maya said, nodding a dignified greeting to Jewel and me.

"Good morning, Maya." I smiled. It had been quite a while since I saw her. The familiar clicking of the beads in her hair as she moved was comforting.

"I wanted to check in on you, in light of everything. How's class going?" Maya asked.

"Class is, well, class. It's going, I suppose," I said.

"That good?" She laughed softly.

Belleza passed by us and shot a dirty look in my direction before continuing on her way.

"I see things are just the same as when I went here," Maya said under her breath. It was funny thinking of Maya being my age and dealing with mean classmates. "Is she giving you a lot of trouble?"

I giggled. "No, not really. Plus, Jewel here is great at protecting me." I winked at Jewel, and she puffed out her chest with pride.

"Well, I will let you get going to your classes. I'll be around a bit more. Reach out if you need," she said, adjusting her shirt. "Oh, yes, that reminds me, Agathin was asking about you. You should take time to visit her soon."

Jewel and I entered the building and parted ways. I went to my classroom, glancing in the open doors as I passed them. Although the academy halls were quiet this morning, more rooms were being used down by my classroom than usual. I entered the classroom and went to the podium.

"Same thing as usual," Mr. Sean called from behind a bookshelf. He seemed more kind toward me these days. His voice was tainted with less disappointment.

Right, find the green ball. I frowned. I still was stuck on the same old task as before. I had been able to see the ball multiple times, but not once did I see where it was located. I took a look at the journal still propped open on the podium, hoping it would reveal some secret I hadn't seen before; that would give me an idea of what I was doing wrong. After accepting that the book had no more hints to give, I took my usual spot on the floor. I went through the steps, just as I always did. I rested my hands in my lap, just brushing the floor with my knuckles. Nothing happened. For an hour, I sat there. I was starting to think that I would be doing this lesson for the rest of my days. The green ball was just there to taunt me.

Mr. Sean came around the corner and sighed. "Esmari, you've been on this task for weeks."

"I know, sir." I looked down at the ground. *Don't remind me.*

"How is it that you could tell me the ball color on day one, but nothin' now?"

"I just see the ball. That's it," I muttered.

"You have to control your power!" he said, his voice laced with agitation.

"I'm trying—"

"Try harder. Tell me where the ball is!" He demanded.

My ears were hot. *Can't you see that I'm trying?* I clenched my jaw holding back tears.

"Where is it? Tell me! Show me!"

"I don't know!" I cried out, slamming my hands into the floor.

My surroundings disappeared. I could see a figure. A woman. *She's stacking something on a shelf. She's turned away. The shelf is rocking—*

Everything faded back into view. "It's going to fall!" I gasped as I jumped to my feet. I ran to the door and swung it open, racing into the hall. I remembered seeing the woman earlier in a classroom nearby, but where? My heart pounded.

CRASH!

The sound came from just a few doors down from where I was.

"No, no, no, no, no," I muttered, running to the sound. I could hear footsteps close behind me, but I didn't turn to see who it was. All I could think about was that woman. I nearly slid into the doorway and looked around frantically.

The woman glanced up at me and then back down at the shelf now on the ground beside her.

She had one hand on her chest and the other on her hip. "Well, that was a close one!" she huffed.

I let out a sigh of relief. "You're okay?"

She patted herself down for a moment and nodded. "Yeah, I'm okay."

"Good," I said, barely audible, my heart still pounding in my ears.

I turned to find Mr. Sean looking down at me with a face of stone. There was anger in his eyes. He didn't say a word. He lifted a hand, snagged the shoulder of my shirt, and ushered me away.

Through the halls, we marched. I stumbled to keep up with his long, uneven stride. We made it to the lobby and didn't slow down, passing a confused looking Belleza along the way. I didn't have time to think about what she possibly could be thinking of me. Up the stairs, Mr. Sean dragged me, taking two at a time, then down the hall to the very end. Mr. Higgens' office. Mr. Sean flung open the door and shoved me in, finally letting go of me.

"She's a Mind Sight," he sneered at a shocked Mr. Higgens with one arm jutted out, pointing at me. My breath caught in my throat.

"She—How do you know?" Mr. Higgens asked, trying to calm his voice.

"She is a Mind Sight," he hissed, enunciating each word. Mr. Higgens glanced at me for a moment, then back at Mr. Sean.

"Sean—" Mr. Higgens began.

"I refuse to teach her!"

"But, Sean—" Mr. Higgens stammered.

"I said, I refuse!" Mr. Sean barked and stormed out of the room, slamming the door behind him.

I was scared. My hands trembled. I felt like crumpling up into a ball. *Had I done something wrong?* I recounted what all had just happened. *I don't understand what was so terrible. Wait, did he say I was a Mind Sight? What happened to me being a Distance Sight?* I felt sick and lost. I looked at Mr. Higgens, who was staring at the desk. I searched his face for answers, for some kind of reassurance as it felt like the world was falling apart around me. He finally took a deep long breath and picked up his phone.

"Hi, it's Higgens—I'm good—Yes—Well, something's changed—Right—Sean has refused Esmari—Yes—Yes—No, he says she's a Mind Sight—Right—Is there anyone—Right—Okay—Thank you, goodbye."

He folded his hands and rested them against his chin, his elbows propped on the desk. He sighed and dropped his hands to his lap. I felt smaller and smaller with each passing moment. *Why wasn't he saying anything? Why wouldn't look at me?* A tear of fear and frustration rolled down my cheek. My ears hummed from the silence in the room.

"Well, we've never—but, I'd have to— she would—" Mr. Higgens muttered to himself, deep in thought.

I couldn't take it anymore. "Will you look at me? What did I do wrong?" I shouted. Mr. Higgens looked at me. He wasn't angry that I yelled at him, mostly surprised, I think.

His face softened into a pity filled smile, and said, "Esmari, you didn't do anything wrong, child."

"Then why does he refuse to teach me?" I pleaded.

"Please understand, there are events of the past that affect him heavily. Why don't you take the rest of the day off of studying? Come see me when you get here tomorrow morning," Mr. Higgens said calmly.

I stood in shock for another moment over everything. Slowly, I nodded, wiping the tears from my chin with the back of a still trembling hand. I left the office and dragged myself down the stairs. I felt numb and confused, meandering my way out the door. The clouds in the sky were gray, and there was a humid weight about the atmosphere. I let my feet wander along with my mind and just walked. I didn't have a location I was headed.

Before long, I realized I had walked all the way to the beach. A wave of anger rose inside my chest. Hot tears streamed down my face. I had guilt in my gut, but for what? All I wanted to do was go away. I flittered my wings and smeared the tears from my eyes with the palms of my hands. I darted off, flying as fast as I could as if I were leaving my feelings behind. Faster and faster and faster, until I was breathing heavy and needed a break. I looked down to find a rock platform and landed there. I sat down and wrapped my arms around my knees.

"Gosh, Esmari. You fly fast," breathed a familiar voice as they landed beside me. I looked up to see Maya peering down at me. She sat beside me and looked out onto the water.

"Why are you here?" I mumbled.

She sighed. "Agathin told me. Would you like to talk?"

"I just don't know what I did wrong. One minute, I'm in the classroom with a teacher who finally didn't hate my existence. Then the next, he's disowning me," I said, letting out a big grunt and letting my knees catch my forehead.

"You really didn't know?" she asked softly. For a moment, there was a slight pity in her voice.

I lifted my head a little and stared out at the rock in front of me. "I mean, I guess part of me knew that I wasn't getting anywhere with the

Distance Sight lessons. But I thought I was just late to catch on, like how I was late to get my wings. But, no. That wasn't it at all. Now, I'm being told I'm a Mind Sight! I wasn't even doing the correct lessons! And Mr. Sean has treated me like I'm a terrible being. It's not like I have control over what power I have. And that's another thing, I can't even control it!" I rambled through angry sobs.

Maya sat quietly and just listened. Part of me wanted her to advise me, but I think she knew I just needed to vent it all out.

"How am I supposed to learn, if I don't even have a teacher?" I continued. "What if I can't learn how to control my ability? What then? I already can feel its strength. But what's a Mind Sight anyway? Am I really such a terrible person for being one? Or is it just Mr. Sean hating me that much? Why did he suddenly refuse me? Isn't it a good thing that we know what my Sight is? So, I can learn it properly?"

"Esmari, it's not you. Mr. Sean has only ever taught one Mind Sight before. And it didn't end well. Please, don't ask me to explain any more than that, okay? Just understand that it's not you," Maya said. Her tone was more comforting than usual, but still had that dignified, proper quality about it.

I nodded and took a breath of the salty air. A cool breeze sent a chill through my spine. Maya stood and extended a hand out to me. I took it and stood as well. She paused for a moment and looked to the clouded sky.

"It looks like rain," she noted. "I'm going to get going. Don't get stuck out in the rain."

I watched her fly off for a moment. She had such a smooth and confident way about her when she flew. I flittered up into the sky just as it started to drizzle. Quickly, I headed for The Dripping Crown. I stepped inside as it began to downpour. *The weather really matches my mood.* The thought brought a smirk to my face, though it didn't make me feel any better. I plopped down at the counter and rested my head on my arms. I was exhausted, both emotionally and physically. I heard the sound of a cup meeting the counter near me. Slowly, I looked up to see a large mug with a great big dollop of whipped cream bouncing on top, and on the other side of the counter, Victor was resting his chin against his arms, peering back at me.

"Bad day?" he whispered.

"Yeah," I breathed and nodded toward the door. "I'm waiting out the rain."

"Okay. I'll make you something to eat," he said.

A few minutes later, he returned with a toasted sandwich. He slid it in front of me and walked away without a word, giving me my space. I finished what I could of the sandwich and drank the delicious hot coffee drink he left me. I played with the rim of the empty mug for a long while, until Victor finally took it away from me.

When the rain let up, I headed for the dorms. It was afternoon by the time I stepped foot in the building. There were whispers all around me as I passed different groups of people. Upstairs, I ran into the last person I wanted to see at that very moment. Belleza and her smug-looking face.

"Rough day?" Belleza said, pouting a fake lip at me. It was disconcerting how willing she was to kick me when I was down.

"Not now, Belleza," I said, trying to go around her. She stepped in front of me again, blocking my way.

"Rumor has it that your teacher isn't your teacher anymore," she smirked. Kasius slipped by us, glancing at me slightly as he passed. My eyes followed him for a moment. "You really should stay away from Kasius."

"Why does it matter to you?" I asked, trying to calm the burning agitation in my throat.

"You have no right to be around him. You have no right even being here. You're a dirt head that no teacher wants as their student. You're a danger to everyone here. A Royal without a teacher to help them properly control their power is like a ticking time bomb. And I don't want my Kasius to be in the way when it all blows up," she sassed.

Anger brewed inside me. I glared at her and swallowed back the jumble of nasty words bubbling up in my throat. *Don't stoop to her level, Es.*

Suddenly, a firm hand gripped my wrist and pulled me away. I looked up to see the striking profile of Kasius beside me, pulling me along. A few strides later, his hand relaxed, and he released my arm. He looked at the ground and just stood still.

"You know, helping me like that might make Belleza see you as an enemy," I said. He shoved a hand in his pocket and strode off.

I smiled softly. I was grateful for the gesture. My anger was getting the best of me, and I wasn't sure what I would have said or done. I knocked on Jewel's door, and she opened it right away with a half-eaten apple in her mouth and armful of snacks.

"Es!" she greeted, pulling the apple from her mouth. I followed her inside and shut the door behind me. We sat down in our usual spots. "Okay, so, I heard rumors today. Tell me what happened? Did Mr. Sean really refuse to continue teaching you? I want the whole story."

I grunted and looked at her curious eyes. I explained everything to her. From the exercise, to the woman, to being thrown into the Head of the

Academy's office without a decent explanation. After I was done, she just sat still. She mulled over the information in her head. Finally, she looked up at me.

"Okay," she said, standing. "Zoning out to loud music it is."

She nodded at me definitively and flipped the on switch of the stereo. We lounged back in the bean bags, not talking for hours. Just letting the music drown out our thoughts. She didn't ask anything anymore. Periodically, we would pass a snack bag back and forth. But that was it. And surprisingly, it was just what I needed.

thirteen

The next morning, I woke up on Jewel's floor, where I had fallen asleep the night before. Groggy, I sat up and listened to the silence for a moment. A flood of memories from the day before rushed in. My heart sank into my stomach at the thought of having to face the day. I didn't want to get up. I wanted so badly to go back to sleep until everything was right again. *No, you can face this.*

I stood up and twisted my hair up into a bun.

Looking in the mirror on Jewel's wall, I gently touched my necklace and reminisced about my shopping trip with Mom. I hadn't taken the necklace off since that day, and now it seemed like one of the few things that felt right. I didn't understand who I was, but feeling the stone of the necklace in my hands gave me a confidence I couldn't describe.

"Morning," Jewel said, taking a big stretch. "You look almost ready to go! Hang on, I'll join you." She stumbled out of bed and fetched a pair of socks to wear.

"I'm going to go change really quick," I said, forcing a smile.

"Okay, okay, I'll be out in a minute then!" she said, rushing to the bathroom and smoothing down her hair with her fingers nearly tripping along the way.

I left her room and turned to unlock my door, stopping in my tracks. In large, bold letters the words "You don't belong dirt head" were written on my door. I didn't recognize the writing, but I had an idea of who it might have been. A moment later, Jewel rushed out of her door.

"I thought you were going to change—" She had turned to see the door as well. "Aw, now come on! What are we? Five-year-olds? Who even does this anymore?"

I sighed. "It's fine. Let's just go."

"No! I want to know who did this!" she called out, her voice echoing in the hall. Some people peaked out of their dorms and looked in our direction.

"Jewel, please, I just want to go," I pleaded with her. I pulled at her arm, and she frowned, letting out a sigh. I looked around at all the people now staring at us and ducked my head down, feeling embarrassed.

"Yeah, okay, let's go," she agreed, linking her arm with mine.

Jewel walked with me all the way to Mr. Higgens' office.

"Want me to go in with you?" she asked.

I wanted more than anything to tell her yes, but I didn't want her to be late to her class. "No, it's okay," I smiled.

"Okay, see you at lunch?" She offered. I nodded. She gave my arm a quick squeeze and retreated back down the hallway, leaving me on my own to enter the Head of the Academy's office. I gave a lite tap on the door.

"Come in," Mr. Higgens beckoned. I entered and closed the door with a now trembling hand. Mr. Higgens stood from his chair behind his desk and nodded, leaning heavily against his cane. "Good morning, Esmari."

"Good morning, sir," I greeted. Mr. Sean was slouched in a nearby chair, just as he was the first day I met him. I carefully joined in the accompanying chair, feeling nervous and uncomfortable.

"I will get right to it then. Mr. Sean has chosen for the time being to cease being your teacher. I will respect that. However, Esmari has every right to continue to learn here at the school. I will not deny her that. And you know more than anyone how crucial it is for Esmari to learn to control her abilities. Being that we don't have any other teachers in Sight Power, Esmari, I have decided to allow you to do independent study. The materials in the Sight classroom will be available to you to learn from. You both will share the space. But, understand that since Mr. Sean refuses to teach you, you are truly going to be learning on your own. No one else on this campus will be able to help you, because there are no other Sights. So please, Esmari, be careful with trying new lessons and exercises, don't overestimate your abilities," Mr. Higgens lectured, pacing as he spoke. His cane clicked against the floor rhythmically with his words.

"Thank you, sir," I said. A sense of momentary relief washed over me.

Mr. Sean said nothing. He simply stood and

left the room. I sat for a moment longer before thanking Mr. Higgens again and leaving the room. In a daze, I walked through the halls to the classroom. By the time I arrived, Mr. Sean had already locked himself away in his office. I looked around at all the books sitting on the shelves in the room and felt overwhelmed. How was I supposed to know where to start?

"Well, you gotta start somewhere, Es," I said to myself, trying to give myself even the smallest amount of reassurance.

Taking a breath, I began skimming the shelves for books that remotely mentioned Mind Sight. I gathered books and journals on history and general lessons on Sights. I was starting from square one, and I hated the feeling it gave me. The more books I thumbed through, the less confident I felt about the independent study idea. Before, Mr. Sean didn't teach me in the traditional sense, but he at least would give me the correct materials. At one point in my searching, I came across the green ball sitting smugly in the corner of a shelf.

"Oh, now I find you," I scoffed.

By noon, I had a pretty hefty stack of books to begin with. I stacked them by the podium and exited to the cafeteria. It was crowded today. Most everyone's eyes were glancing at me. I could hear whispers forming around me like smoke filling the air. I kept my head down and got my lunch. Finding an empty table, I saved a seat for Jewel, who, thankfully, joined me a few minutes later.

"So, this is what it's like to be popular!" Jewel joked.

"Everyone is talking about me, aren't they?" I said.

"Yep," she said, cracking the seal on her juice bottle. I groaned. She smiled at me. "So, what's the verdict? What did Mr. Higgens say? I mean, obviously, you're still allowed to be here. But, you know, how are things going to proceed from now on?"

"Independent study," I shrugged as I pushed a grape around on my plate with my fork.

"Whoa. I didn't know they allowed that. Interesting," Jewel pondered, taking a big gulp of her juice.

"Yeah, at first, I was almost relieved. A bit excited about my freedom. But I realized I have no clue what I am doing. Not that I really had much of a clue before, but now," I sighed. "Now, I really don't understand."

"So?"

"So, now I'm a Mind Sight," I said.

"Okay, so what? You're a Mind Sight? It's just a different title to your ability. It doesn't change your ability. You were getting somewhere before, right? But you were just, I don't know, focusing on it the wrong way. So, you just have to figure it out. And you can actually put your effort into the correct lessons, right?" Jewel said. She made it seem so easy.

"Yeah, I suppose you're right," I said.

"You know I'm right," she said confidently. "I mean take me, for example. I couldn't shower for, like, two weeks when I was first learning my ability. The water just didn't work the right way."

I laughed. "Seriously?"

"Yeah," she winced, remembering it. "It was not a fun time."

"That's gross," I teased.

"It really was," she agreed with a laugh. "But now look at me! Able to control my ability, and more importantly, clean and odor-free!"

I chuckled at her.

After lunch, we cleaned up our trays and headed back to our classrooms. I entered the room and left a muffin and a bottle of juice by Mr. Sean's closed office door. I was fairly certain he hadn't eaten anything but a snack bar yet again today. I went to the podium and picked up the journal from before, this time turning to the pages labeled for Mind Sight. I found it to have much less specific information than the pages about Distance Sights, which was a little disappointing.

A couple of books weren't as relevant to Mind Sights as I thought they were, while a few seemed like something a bit too advanced for me to try at the moment. I went back to the journal and read it through. A passage stuck out to me, and I found myself re-reading it a few times over.

Many Sights, especially Mind Sights, keep an item on them at all times. Something special to them. The item is usually worn or kept in a pocket and is often small. For example, a ring or a single card. It can help to ground them and calm them in overwhelming times. Some Sight episodes can cause the person to lose time or spatial awareness. Having an item that they can physically touch helps to re-center them after the episode is done. It can also help a Sight enter into an episode.

I stood for a moment and pondered this. Out of habit, I adjusted my necklace on my neck. I smiled to myself. *I guess this is your item, Es.* I gently dragged my fingertips against the chain and rubbed my tired eyes, glancing at the clock.

"I think that's enough for today." I decided.

I stepped away from the podium and looked down to the office, where the muffin and juice still sat, untouched, in front of the door. I frowned and shook my head, leaving the room. Quietly, I walked through the halls of the school. It was almost peaceful in the building at this hour. Some classes had already been dismissed for the day, while a few students remained behind working on open labs or projects.

I made my way back to the dorms. It was a warmer day today than it was yesterday, and the late afternoon sun left a comforting warmth on my tired shoulders. Several groups of students were utilizing the benches outside and enjoying the weather. I climbed the stairs of my building and rounded the corner, heading to my dorm. I watched my feet against the floor as I stepped, barely looking up by the time I reached my door.

I gasped and looked around the empty halls. My door was clean. No words left on it, not even a trace of what had been there before. It was so clean, that it looked almost new. Baffled, I smiled to myself and entered in.

———

By the end of the week, the whispering about me had stopped, and things went mostly back to normal. Each day, I read about anything that seemed to have to do with my power. Mr. Sean hadn't said a word to me, though, nor did he ever take the food I brought back from lunch for him.

But I still kept bringing it in case he was to change his mind. I had yet to try any exercises that I had read about, feeling like I wanted a firm foundation on what exactly I was aiming to accomplish.

"Es, you're quiet today," Hunter said to me that evening at the coffee shop.

"Just tired, I suppose."

"You are really wearing yourself thin studying," he noted. "How's it going anyway?"

I shrugged at him. "How's the carpentry going?"

"It's going so great. Hank came by the class again and said that depending on how I do on my end of course exam next month, he's interested in maybe taking me in as an apprentice. A paid apprentice!" he said with glee. His eyes twinkled with the dream.

"That's amazing! Crazy to think that you are already finishing that beginner's carpentry course up." I shook my head. It didn't feel like we had been here in Banshui for that long.

"I know, right? Finn was accepted for an apprenticeship, too. We were both talking about maybe looking for a place to rent together. Maybe with Darren and Moz. It's just an idea at this point, but I think it would be so cool."

I sipped the rest of my coffee and placed the cup next to me on the floor. Leaning back on my hands, I sighed. Everything around me faded. *A woman is laughing, she's bumped her mug—* My surrounding came back. I swallowed hard and rubbed at my neck. Out of the corner of my eye, I saw Hunter search my face for a moment. The sound of a shattering mug from downstairs made the both of us jump.

"What the—" Hunter gasped.

"It was a mug," I said.

"You still don't have any control of your power, do you?" he asked cautiously.

"No," I sighed. "No, I don't."

"It's okay, Es. You'll get it. I believe in you," he encouraged.

"Thanks," I said. My stomach growled. "What I wouldn't give for one of Mom's muffins right about now."

"Yeah," Hunter said. Suddenly, his expression changed to a big smile. "Hey, you know what? I think there are still a few of the muffins in our fridge that Finn's parents brought by. I know it's not the same, but they're good. What do you say we head to my dorm?"

We cleaned up our area and headed outside. There was a soft breeze blowing in from the coast, making the air feel almost magical. I itched to fly. With a smirk, I faced Hunter.

"Race you to your dorm!" I challenged then

fluttered up into the sky, not waiting for Hunter to answer.

"Hey! No fair! We already know you are way faster!" Hunter laughed from behind me.

We soared across the sky over Banshui. I took in the rush; the incredible feeling of my wings cutting through the air. I listened to the whoosh that each of my wings made as they flapped. I was free. Even if it was just a moment of serenity. Letting go of the stress with each breath.

Landing just in front of the dorm, I panted with exhaustion and enjoyed the moment of bliss. Hunter joined me and flopped onto the ground. He laid back and closed his eyes, his chest rising and falling as he caught his breath. He opened his mouth as if to say something, but couldn't. One eye open, and looking in my direction, he lifted a finger and pointed at me, shaking his head. I laughed and held out a hand to help him up. He took ahold of my outstretched arm and yanked me down to the ground with him. We both sat for a moment, laughing. It felt like old times back in Athra.

When we both finally calmed ourselves down, we got up and headed inside. There were several small groups of people inside the lobby of the dorm. Lots of chatter echoed through the room.

"Hunter!" Finn called, jogging over to us.

"What's going on?" Hunter asked, his

eyebrows furrowing with confusion.

"They caught an Ex," Finn said. Hunter and I both looked at each other in surprise. "Yeah, I guess it was like he wanted to be caught. He was saying something about being here to pass along a message. He said that his leader was interested in someone here who had the right potential."

"What does that even mean?" I asked.

"I don't know, but there's talk about the attack not being random," Finn said.

"Well, from what I understand, they don't like Non-Royals. So, why are they threatening you guys, then talking about needing someone with potential? They most likely are here for a Royal, right?" I said, trying to piece it together.

"Maybe they are trying to lure someone out by doing that. Like make them angry or something?" Hunter pondered

"Yeah, could be. I don't know. You guys just need to keep your heads down. Stay safe. It doesn't seem like this is the last of it. It seems like another warning to me. And whoever they are interested in, probably already knows. So just watch out for each other, okay?" I said. My heart hurt just thinking of the two of them being caught up in all of this.

"You act like we don't already do that! Hunter, why does she belittle us so?" Finn wined, throwing an arm around Hunter's shoulder and staring up at the ceiling thoughtfully.

"Finn, I just don't know. These Royals, these women, I just will never understand their ways!" Hunter played along.

I rolled my eyes. "You're both children. I'm talking to children," I laughed with a shrug and tossing my hands up with defeat.

"And now the Royal calls us children!" Finn gawked. Hunter pretended to sob into his hands. "Have you no kindness in your heart?"

I sighed to myself, shaking my head with a chuckle. "I'm going to head home."

"Fine! Be gone with you, Royal!" Finn demanded sarcastically, flashing me an attempt at a stern face. Hunter snorted, and we all broke into laughter.

I waved them goodbye and headed back to my dorm building. A wisp of air kissed my cheek. It was a beautiful afternoon that, for once, I didn't want to spend cooped up inside my room. I wandered the area until I found a shady weeping willow tree to relax under. Laying back in the soft grass with my eyes closed, I just listening to the world.

My mind wandered from one thing to the next. I thought about the Ex who was caught. I thought about the way flying made me feel. I explored ideas of how to try controlling my Mind Sight. My thoughts danced through the different materials I had read on my power. I could feel something inside me, my power, aching to be used. I laced my fingers in the grass, feeling each blade catch on the ridges of my fingerprints. I felt the slightly damp soil just barely at the bottom of the grass. It was cool against my palms and ground its way underneath each of my fingernails. I heard footsteps near me fading. *High heels, light step, uneven rhythm, elegant figure. Second woman a step behind. Belleza, Lilly. They are exchanging looks.*

I opened my eyes just as something wet doused my face. For a moment, I couldn't get my bearings. *Was I still in a Mind Sight episode?* I grabbed for my necklace and felt its small stone in my fingers. I let out a sigh.

"Oopsie. I'm sorry," Belleza said, sticking out her fat lower lip in a mocking way. Lilly giggled and faked a frown. Her phony voice made my jaw clench. "I didn't see you there."

I paused for a moment and centered my emotions. Sitting up, I looked at her and gently wiped the water from my face. I looked at her stance. She leaned slightly more weight on one foot than the other. Tilting my head with a smirk, I said, "Your right leg is shorter than your left, you know."

She looked flustered. Letting out an offended,

almost embarrassed, scoff she turned her nose up at me and hurried away, dragging a very confused Lilly along with.

"So, how did you know?" Kasius asked from the opposite side of the tree.

How long had he been there? "She walks uneven," I answered, though I got the feeling that he already knew it himself. I heard him breathe a quiet chuckle. My stomach growled. *I never did get a muffin back at Hunter's dorm.*

I heard a rusting and looked back to see Kasius taking out a packaged pastry from his backpack sitting beside him. He scooted around the trunk of the tree, coming closer to me, and held it out, nodding for me to take it. I smiled timidly and accepted the blueberry filled pastry offering. He reached into his bag again and retrieved two juices. He looked at the flavors for a moment and handed one to me. Mango. I paused for a second and looked at his face. He opened his bottle and took a sip. Leaning his back against the tree trunk, he looked out to the sky. *Had he been the one to save me the juice at the cafeteria that day?*

"Thank you," I said finally. Unwrapping the pastry, I took a bite. "You know, if you are seen with me, people might talk."

I looked over at his unfazed face. He said nothing, just lifted his juice to his lips and took another sip. The light shone through the leaves of the trees and glistened on the burgundy in his hair.

"You don't care, do you?" I said softly.

The corner of his lips curled. "Nope."

An uneasy guilt still sat in my gut. *You're friends with Belleza, who seems to hate me.* "Why are you kind to me?" I asked. He turned to look at me, his mesmerizing black eyes peering right at mine. I felt embarrassed by the way he looked at me.

"You're different," he smiled, then turned back to the sky.

"Different," I repeated with a chuckle. "That's one accurate description."

He turned his whole body to face me now. "Why do you say it like that?" His question was genuine.

"I just—" I started, then shook my head. *Spare him the sob story, Esmari.* I crumpled up the sticky wrapper from the pastry in my hands. "I'm sure you have better things to do than listen to me talk about my pitiful life."

"Esmari, I've got time," he assured.

I swallowed and thought for a moment, his gaze stayed on me as he waited. "Well, I guess I've just always been different. When everyone else in my class got their wings, I didn't. I had begun to think they wouldn't ever come. I wanted to get my wings so I could be normal. I wanted to fit in. Then when I finally got my wings, I still was different. The way they look is different. Like something is wrong with them. The way I felt with them was different. I started to have Sight episodes. I didn't know what they were at the time, but I knew it wasn't normal. I knew I wasn't like the others in Athra. When Maya told me I was a Royal, I was excited. I thought I'd be with others like me, I wouldn't be different. I would fit in, and I'd blend in. But, I'm a Sight, a Mind Sight at that, who can't control her own power and who's teacher denied her," I babbled. Leaning my head back against the tree, I let out a slow sigh, still in thought. I winced, realizing I had just rattled off my whole life story in one fell swoop. *I have been spending way too much time with Jewel.* Taking in a big breath, I glanced at Kasius, who was patiently listening to me. "And now you think I'm pathetic, I'm sure."

He smiled at me with a twinkle in his eye. "You care too much about what others think."

"Oh, gee. That's what you got out of that?" I smirked, speaking half under my breath, taking a sip of the juice.

"If you always try to fit in and be like everyone else, you will never discover what you are capable of," Kasius said it in such a way that made my breath catch. I looked away and fiddled with my necklace.

"I suppose you're right," I sighed. "Maybe, that's what's holding me back with my power."

He shrugged gently but offered no advice. We listened to another breeze whistle through the blades of grass. After a moment in comfortable silence, he gathered his backpack and zipped it back up. I fiddled with the lid of the juice bottle, running my nail against its grooves. From the corner of my eye, I could see him smile softly again as he looked at my face once more.

"Do you want me to walk you in?" he asked.

I paused in thought. "No, I think I'd like to enjoy the fresh air a little longer."

He nodded to me and swung his bag over his shoulder. Swiftly he turned and strode off toward the dorm building. I smiled to myself and laid my head back against the tree again. Closing my eyes, I let my thoughts drift away with the afternoon breeze.

fourteen

It had been a few days since the Ex was caught, and there was an unsettling feeling in the air. On one hand, many people seemed happy that they caught the one who left the threats, but on the other hand, the warning he spoke of left an eerie stain in the air. There were rumors about who they were interested in. It seemed like the only thing that people talked about, almost as common as talking about the weather or what you were going to have for lunch.

Jewel and I found time that warm morning to visit with Agathin, and we invited Maya to come along, to which she happily accepted. Jewel was giddy with the opportunity to tag along and "finally meet *the* Agathin," as she put it. She continually was adjusting her clothing and rambling about what an opportunity it was while we waited for Maya just outside the doors of Agathin's office.

"Daddy was talking with some of the Authoritative Elders he works with, and he thinks that whoever they are interested in has got to be strong in their power," Belleza said to Lilly as they walked. I could see them approaching where we were standing. I soaked in the mid-day heat and cringed at our inevitable encounter.

"What do you think?" Lilly asked her, wide-eyed.

"Well, I think solid crowns like us tend to be more skilled in our abilities. These sightings and threats didn't start until recently, after we were at the academy. I'm not saying it could be one of us, but you didn't see the way that man was looking at me." She pouted and ticked her tongue. Jewel and I rolled our eyes at each other.

"Lezzy, you've got to be careful! Your power is getting stronger by the day, what if you're a target of theirs?" Lilly wined.

"I know, it's so scary to think about," Belleza sighed. She looked up to see both Jewel and I listening to their conversation. "I guess you two should feel lucky. At least you don't have these worries. I almost envy you. Almost."

She let out a cackle, and Jewel stepped toward her with her fist clenched. My chest burned with agitation, and I felt a tingle in my fingertips from something within that I couldn't quite understand. Slowly, I took a breath and calmed myself. Jewel, on the other hand, continued to glare at her with fire in her eyes.

"You—" she growled.

I snagged her arm. "Jewel, don't," I breathed.

Belleza and Lilly giggled as they walked away. Jewel huffed a frustrated sigh and twisted her face into an angry frown.

"One day, I want to give her a piece of—a piece of—" Jewel stammered, completely flustered. "A piece of my mind! She just thinks that she is so cool and everyone envies her! So, what?"

Maya joined us. Leaning over to me, she whispered, "Is she okay?"

"Yeah, give her a minute," I said back.

"What! You can move liquid and stuff! That makes you so great, Belleza?" Jewel continued, not noticing Maya's arrival.

"That rude classmate of yours?" Maya asked

me. I nodded.

"Well, news flash! You're not the first! And certainly, won't be the last! So, you can just take your solid crown and fly off!" Jewel fumed. She huffed out another sigh and collected herself. "Oh, hi, Maya!"

Maya smirked at her sudden change in demeanor. "Hello. If you're ready?" she said, motioning to the door.

"Oh, oh, yeah, I'm good," Jewel said, opening the door for us.

We went straight into the building to the tinted windows, and Maya pulled the red string to buzz for Agathin. We waited a moment. No one came to let us in. Maya grew impatient and pulled the string again. A second later, the door swung open.

"I am an old woman. It takes me a moment to get to the door, you know!" Agathin scolded teasingly. She saw Maya and me, and her face lit up with excitement. I glanced at Jewel, who looked like a child seeing the stars for the first time.

"Hello, Agathin," I smiled.

"Esmari! It's been quite some time! And you've brought a friend with too!" Agathin exclaimed, clasping her hands together, her deep navy colored shawl swaying on the crooks of her arms.

Jewel stepped forward and stood with pride. "My name is Jewelei, Ms. Agathin, ma'am," she said, sticking out a confident hand to shake.

"Hello, dear," Agathin said, grasping her hand. "Please, none of that Ms. Or ma'am stuff. Just Agathin will do just fine."

Jewel giggled bashfully and tucked a stray piece of hair behind her ear. "Okay, Agathin it is."

We followed her back to the seating area. Jewel plopped down and looked around the office with amazement plastered on her face. I glanced at Maya as she relaxed back into a chair, looking exhausted. The dark circles under her eyes were even more visible in the bright light of the office. Agathin looked at her, too, and frowned slightly.

"Where's my Binbin today?" she asked.

"He's visiting with a friend, I think," Maya answered.

"Maya, you had better be careful when you are exercising your power. You're not overdoing it, right?" Agathin cautioned.

Maya sighed. "I'm fine."

Agathin ticked her tongue at her. She turned to me and looked me over. "And your studies, Esmari? How are they going, now that you are doing them independently?"

"I'm—" I started, carefully considering my choice of words. "I'm reading everything I can get my hands on. I've learned a lot of history so far."

"I see," Agathin said, pursing her lips. "And

Mr. Sean?"

"He's currently still ignoring me," I said, looking to the side.

"Oh, he'll come around. I'm sure," Agathin said, adjusting her shawl onto her shoulders, covering what I could barely see of her wings on her back. "Jewelei, what power do you have, dear?"

Jewel lit up, excited that her moment had finally come. "Well, I can hold liquid," she said. She grabbed a small bottle of water that was sitting on the side table beside her. "It's easier if I just show you."

"Please do!" Agathin said cheerily.

Jewel smiled a great big grin and twisted the cap off of the water bottle. Maya sat forward in her chair to also see what Jewel was about to show. She glanced at me and then back at Agathin, before pouring a small amount of the water in her hand. Carefully, she set the bottle down and began to shape the water into a ball as if it were clay. Her power had definitely improved a bit. She then stretched it between her fingers a few times, giggling at the squishing sound it made, before returning it back to the bottle.

Agathin applauded her. "That's wonderful. You really seem to have great control over it."

Jewel grinned widely. "Thank you," she said,

and I gave her a reassuring nudge.

"And your parents, Jewelei, did you inherit your power from one of them?" Agathin asked.

"Yeah, my dad has a similar power. My mom is a Non-Royal. So, she doesn't have power. Of course, that's what being Non- Royal kind of is, so, I'm sure you came to that conclusion on your own." Jewel rambled.

Agathin chuckled. "Yes, that makes sense. And which district did you grow up in, then?"

"Oh, I'm from the West District. My parents are still there," Jewel noted.

"Oh, Esmari, how's your friend, Hunter, was it?" Agathin asked as she turned her attention once again to me.

"He's doing really well. He found that he's really liking carpentry and is even being considered as an apprentice soon," I explained. Thinking of how happy Hunter had been lately made my heart warm. "Had he not been busy today, I'm sure he would have loved to have joined us for our visit."

"Carpentry, you say?" Agathin smiled. Her mind seemed to be thinking of something else as her eyes wandered down to the small coffee table sitting between us.

"What is it, Agathin?" Maya said, noticing her look as well.

She looked back up at us with kindness in her deep blue eyes. "Oh, nothing. I'm just glad that he wasn't at the building, that no one was at the carpentry building, when the Ex left that awful threat," she said, her voice still trailed with thought.

"Yeah," I sighed. A buzz at the door startled me. It was much louder sounding on the inside of the office than it was standing outside.

"Oh, my," Agathin said, glancing up at the clock on the wall. "My next appointment is here already. Shame that we can't talk longer, ladies."

"It's alright. You sure keep yourself busy," Maya said, shaking her head. Another buzz came from the door, drowning out the clacking from the beads in Maya's hair.

"Honestly, you all forget I am getting on in age!" Agathin said, flustered, beginning to get up.

"We'll let them in on our way out," Maya smiled, patting Agathin's arm. Agathin nodded with a thankful look in her eyes and reached a pale, frail hand to give Maya's hand a comforting squeeze.

"Oh, Esmari, could you do me a favor and drop this off with Mr. Higgens? It would save me a trip over there," Agathin said, handing me an envelope.

"Sure," I nodded.

We found our way out and said our goodbyes to Maya before heading back toward the academy. Jewel and I parted ways, and I headed inside. It was quiet today; most classes were holding optional open labs. It almost felt as though I was unintentionally trespassing as I listened to my muffled footsteps against the burgundy carpeted steps of the staircase. As I turned down the hall to Mr. Higgens' office, I could hear the echoes of an argument. For a moment, I wanted to turn around and come back at another time. I looked down at the letter in my hands once more. *No, you gave your word to Agathin.* Cautiously, I continued down the hall toward the voices.

"You aren't going to say anything?" said a voice I recognized as Mr. Sean.

"She's just a child," Mr. Higgens said.

Mr. Sean grunted in frustration. "Everyone is a child to you. You have no right keeping something like this from her."

"And tell her what?" Mr. Higgens yelled. "That there's a possibility that she might be the target. We don't know that for certain!"

"Great. That's just great!" Mr. Sean scoffed.

"Sean, I'm not going to worry a student about something like that for no reason. There's no telling how she will cope with that kind of information." Mr. Higgens' tried to reason. I could hear the irritation building in his deep voice. "You don't understand."

"She has a strong spirit. She would cope just fine. You know what, you're right. I don't understand. I don't understand why you would keep this from someone and just *hope* they won't be in danger," Mr. Sean sneered. "You know, you haven't changed a bit. For your sake, she better not be a target. Because I know just who to blame if she or anyone else in this ridiculous school gets hurt."

"I am doing what I think is best," Mr. Higgens said. The door swung open, and Mr. Sean stormed out of the office. "Sean!"

Mr. Sean glanced at me for a moment, surprised to see me. He was red with anger. He looked back down at the ground and stomped off. I looked in the office. Mr. Higgens ran his hands over his curly hair and took a breath. Timidly, I tapped on the now open door to the office.

"Yes?" Mr. Higgens sighed then looked up. "Oh, Esmari, come in."

"I'm sorry to bother you, I just came from a visit with Agathin, and she asked me to give you this," I said softly, keeping my head down.

"Ah, yes, thank you," Mr. Higgens smiled, completely disregarding what had happened moments before.

I exited the office and walked down the

hallway. I was still thinking about what I had overheard. *Could Belleza actually have been right? Is she a possible target?* I shook my head at the wild idea and found myself wandering to the classroom. I decided to just spend some time with the books, again.

When I entered, Mr. Sean was already tucked away behind the closed door of his office. I walked along the bookshelves, running my hand against the dusty spines, and searched for some new material to read. When I had found something to my liking, a green book titled "What is power?" in shiny gold, I sat with it on the floor. Something inside urged me to try my power again. One thing was for sure, I was starting to recognize some of the signs.

After I had finished the chapter on the Anatomy of Power, I set the book aside. I thought for a moment, and my mind wandered again about the conversation between Mr. Sean and Mr. Higgens. Shaking my head, I tried to clear my mind. I closed my eyes and felt the ground in front of me. The brick under me was warm from the sun shining in the window. I focused on the texture for a moment, how smooth it was. A twinge surged through the pads of my fingers against the brick. *A male sitting on the floor. Trench coat. Mr. Sean. He's holding a photograph. He looks upset. The picture is blurry —*

A buzzing in my ear started. I opened my eyes and felt the warmth of brick on my cheek. I sat up slowly and rubbed my groggy head. Momentarily, I looked around, trying to get my bearings. I touched my necklace to remind my still slightly spinning head that I was back in reality. When I was ready, I got up and glanced at the clock before heading to the cafeteria.

It was toward the end of the lunch hour when I arrived. Most of the room was empty, aside from a couple of students. I ordered my food and took a seat. My head was still a bit groggy. I cut the large sandwich in two, setting aside one half and an apple for Mr. Sean. I went to open my juice and found myself to still be a bit weak from my Sight episode earlier. I grunted at it, resting it back on the table, and closed my eyes. I felt a presence reach over my shoulder. Startled, I opened my eyes. Kasius cracked open the lid of the juice and set it back in front of me.

"Thanks," I mumbled.

"Have a sip. You're pale," he whispered before sitting at the table just to the right of me.

I rubbed my tense neck, then took a sip of juice. The flavors of bananas and strawberries were intense against my taste buds. It reminded me of the first time I ate after receiving my wings. I smiled to myself at the memory and took another sip. Glancing over, I saw Kasius with his nose, once again, in a book. He seemed peaceful. I took a bite of my sandwich, and my mind wandered. I thought about Hunter and his upcoming exam. I thought about Jewel and her progress with her power. I reminisced on memories of my family back home.

It had grown quiet in the cafeteria, and I decided it was time for me to go back to class. By the time I arrived, I could feel a slight tingle in my fingertips again as an urge to use my Sight grew in me. I shook it off and placed the food for Mr. Sean in front of his closed office door as I always had. *One of these days, you'll accept my food offerings again, Mr. Sean.* I walked over to my usual spot and sat down. A part of me didn't want to use my power again. I still felt off from earlier. But it was almost like having an itch that you have no choice but to scratch.

I placed my fingertips barely on the ground, and instantly my surroundings fell away. *Hunter and Finn, walking, laughing, there's a third laughter, it's not with them, its muddled —*

My surroundings returned just as quickly as they fell away. Reaching for my necklace, I shook my head from the fog and went over what had just occurred in my head. It was the furthest distance away that my Sight had ever taken me. For the first time, it wasn't something in the same building as me. I could still hear the laughter for a moment ringing in my ears. I couldn't tell anything about it, just that it was laced in, almost hidden, with Hunter and Finn's. The idea made me uncomfortable.

I sat for a moment, just relaxing my exhausted mind and body before deciding that I needed to go home and rest. As I stood, I heard the sound of a doorknob clicking in the room. I glanced around toward the office just as Mr. Sean was retreating back inside with the food I left for him in his hands.

fifteen

The days passed by quickly, and, before I knew it, another couple of weeks flew by. With each passing day, I felt my abilities grow more intense inside of me. It had gone from beckoning me with a minor tingle at my fingertips to a growing sensation throughout the veins in my arms. An unsettling sensation that never quite felt satisfied. A sensation that seemed to build and spread the more I used my Mind Sight. Something inside of me still felt uneasy and conflicted, confused almost. Like there was something more I didn't quite understand about it yet. I found the lessons he was gravitating toward were all on the obscure side of things, but it was nice to be challenged. He would focus on one trick, so-to-speak, one day, and then the next, something completely different. But I couldn't help but feel that it was all connected, and I found myself trusting him and his teachings more as the weeks went on.

Mr. Sean had once again begun talking to me, to an extent, that is. A few words here and there, however, it was a start. He still refused to teach me, no matter how much I asked, but his toleration of me was beginning to grow little by little. It was almost starting to feel like a mutual agreement to share the classroom, and the tension in the air was not as thick as it once was.

"Do you plan to stay late today?" Mr. Sean asked me as I re-entered the classroom after lunch.

"Not sure," I noted, tossing him an orange. It was an odd question for him to ask, though I had been staying later than usual these days.

"Mhm," he grunted. He looked more tired than usual.

I couldn't silence my curiosity. "Why?" I asked.

He glanced at me from the corner of his eye, his hands pausing on the half-torn orange peel. He shook his head once and pulled a chunk of the peel off. The boom of thunder echoed in the room, and we both glanced out the window.

"That storm is rolling in," I said under my breath, not entirely sure who I was intending the comment for. He nodded and leaned against the wall, closing his eyes as he ate a slice of the orange.

I went about my studies for a little bit longer, wanting to at least finish the chapter of the book I was on. It talked about abilities and their connections. I learned how some powers can be emotionally driven, and sometimes Royals find their abilities more enhanced when around or focusing on loved ones or friends. Another boom of thunder shook me as I closed up the book. The pitter-patter of the rain against the window made me sigh as I realized I had forgotten to bring a coat or umbrella.

"I suppose I will head out before the storm gets any worse," I said to Mr. Sean, who still remained in the same spot, leaning against the wall. He kept his eyes closed, and half waved to me.

After putting away my materials, I exited the room without another word. I had made it all the way to the lobby by the time I had realized that I left the backpack I brought in for the day sitting in the classroom. For a moment, I stared at the sky, debating if it was worth it to go back or just leave it for tomorrow. I sighed. *Best to get it now, Es.* With a slight pout on my face, I walked my way back down the winding halls to the classroom.

Just as I placed my hand on the door and opened it silently, I heard a muffled sobbing. Mr. Sean sat against the wall with his eyes closed and head leaned back, tears streaming down his face. Tears of sorrow and pain. My heart ached for him, but something deep down in my gut told me he just wanted to be alone. I quietly gathered up my backpack from beside the door and tiptoed out of the classroom.

My thoughts remained on Mr. Sean all the way as I made my journey once again through the academy's winding halls. It was the first time I had seen an emotion out of him other than anger and frustration. I stepped outside into the rain, which seemed to match Mr. Sean's emotions. It was a cool drizzle against my skin, and the sky was clouded over with dark gray. A flash of lightning lit up the sky, and, a moment later, a clap of thunder boomed its response. I had just ducked under a weeping willow tree near my dorm building when the downpour began, leaving me stranded. Jewel came running up behind me, laughing, and completely drenched.

"Well, now! This is quite the storm! So much fun!" She giggled. Using her hand, she squeegeed the water off of her arms and wiped it onto the leaves of a low hanging branch.

"It's not letting up either," I mentioned.

"Let's just make a run for it!" Jewel smiled.

"No—" I detested.

She grinned widely and grabbed my arm. Lightning flashed again. "At the sound of the thunder!" she called out.

A boom of thunder sounded off, and she ran for the dorms, dragging me along behind. Accidentally, she stepped in a puddle and lost her footing, sending the both of us sliding into the squishy mud. A tinge of anger flushed over me, but after taking one look at Jewel, peeling herself out of the mud, the anger vanished. A glob of mud fell off of her chin and splat onto the ground in front of her, sending us both into a roar of laughter. I placed my hands beside me to stabilize myself as I tried to catch my breath. My surroundings vanished from my eyes, but not the sounds around me. As if I had partially triggered my Sight. I could see someone walking toward us, but it was all so blurry. I lifted my hands, and my vision came back. Looking around, I blinked a few times. The sensation it left behind was unsettling for a moment, making me question my own eyesight and hearing. I placed my fingers on my necklace, now completely covered in mud.

"What is it?" Jewel asked. I smiled at her and shook my head.

"Wow," Belleza smirked as she looked down at us. She and Lilly stood completely dry underneath what seemed like an invisible umbrella Belleza was creating for them. "And I don't even get to take the credit for rubbing your faces in mud. You beat me to it."

I felt anger building up inside me. Before I even could think about what I was doing, I took a pile of mud and slung it at Belleza's sparkly white high heels. Jewel's eyes widened just as the mud left my hand, but it was too late. Belleza shrieked and stepped back in disgust. For a moment during this, Belleza accidentally forgot to continue to keep rain off of both her and Lilly, causing Lilly to be instantly drenched. Jewel pressed her lips together to stifle a giggle.

"Lezzy!" Lilly gasped as she pealed her sopping wet hair off of her face. Her mascara was streaming down the cheeks of her dumbfounded expression.

"Don't blame me! Blame her!"

"But my hair!" Lilly wined.

"Your hair? Nobody cares about your hair! Look at what she did to my shoes!" Belleza wined back. Lilly pouted at Belleza's uncaring words toward her. Belleza jutted one very aggravated finger out in my direction. "You—"

"Oh, would you like some more? We can make your skirt to match?" Jewel sassed, lifting a handful of mud. "I hear natural tones are all the rage this season."

"Don't you dare! You two are going to get it!" Belleza said, hurrying off to the dorm with a still pouting Lilly close behind.

Jewel and I giggled and shook our hands from the mud, flinging it on each other as we did so. For a moment, I could have sworn I had seen Lilly glance back, almost envying how silly we were being. I stood and helped Jewel up as well.

"Now, question is, do we stand out here and let the rain wash some of the mud off of us, or head inside?" I pondered with a smile.

Another flash of lightning followed by a clap of thunder close behind rattled in our chest. "I think we should probably head inside," Jewel noted quickly.

We ran inside and straight up to our dorms to clean up, trying our best not to leave a distinct trail behind us. After I had scrubbed completely clean of the mud and put on some dry clothes, I decided to check the lobby for any mail from Athra. I wandered my way downstairs, to the incoming mail slots and was happy to find a letter with my name under my room number.

It was a letter from Bray this time, explaining how he won again in a wing race with his friends. He and Dad had been taking goods to the surrounding towns lately, and he seemed to be enjoying the adventures with Dad more and more. I found myself wandering the halls as I read the letter over. My heart longed for home.

A faint sound of soft music graced the hall. I folded the letter and placed it in my pocket and strolled through the empty halls, admiring the pictures on the walls on the far end of the dorm where I rarely traveled. The music became louder as I approached a dorm room with its door half open. I glanced inside just as the person playing the music stepped into view.

Kasius was swaying as he played the beautifully soothing tone on the violin in his hands. His back was to me. I stopped for a moment, almost entranced as I watched his fingers dance along the strings. My face flushed, realizing I was staring, and I felt as though I was peering in on a private moment. Quietly, I turned away, starting toward my dorm room again.

"Stay," Kasius said, not even missing a beat with the rhythm of his bow. "Please."

He never even turned to me. With a twitch of his pinky finger, the door opened a bit wider. I stepped closer and leaned against his doorframe taking, in the notes of the melody. He continued to sway along and play his violin with such talent and passion. Every so often, his wings would flutter slightly with a wavering note. I felt a warmth growing in my heart as the melody carried on. It filled in the hole of loneliness and the longing for home that sat in my chest. I found myself smiling as the melody concluded with a sweet note fading into the air.

"I hope I didn't intrude," I said softly.

"No, it's been a while since I've had an audience," Kasius smiled as he put his violin back in its case.

"I'm going to head back," I said, nodding toward my dorm room.

"Are you hungry?" he asked suddenly. I nodded sheepishly. "I'll make us something."

He gathered a few ingredients from a small

cabinet inside his dorm, and we headed down the hall to a shared kitchen area. I watched as he began to cook for us. He looked blissful as he sliced some scallions. I tried to offer my help, but he refused with a single shake of his head, leaving me with no choice but to stand helplessly off to the side. It smelled incredible, yet was something I had never seen before.

"Kasius!" Belleza's voice beckoned as she came around the corner. Kasius poured our dinner into the bowls he had set out. "That Esmari. You won't guess what she's done. My shoes are ruined, and it's all her fault!"

Belleza didn't seem to notice I was even there. Kasius looked up at her, and without a word, he looked over at me and raised an eyebrow. I shrugged, feeling embarrassed. He shook his head and chuckled quietly, returning his attention to the bowls.

"What— what are you doing here?" Belleza fumed. She looked at me, then at the two bowls now sitting in front of Kasius. Her jaw clenched, and she stormed off.

Kasius and I sat on the bar seats at the counter. He placed the bowls of food in front of us and handed me a spoon and some chopsticks. I looked at the chopsticks feeling awkward. I had never learned how to eat with them before. Kasius smiled.

"I'll teach you," he said.

How did he know? "Okay," I breathed. I watched him carefully and attempted my best to follow. With the help of both the spoon and chopsticks, I was able to retrieve a noodle from the bowl. It was delicious.

"You cook, and you play violin well. I had no idea," I said, slurping up another bite.

"You didn't ask," he said plainly.

"Would you have told me if I had?" I asked. He shrugged. "That's what I thought. So, where'd you learn to cook?"

"Do you like it?"

"Yeah, it's really, really good," I smiled. "Anything else you are good at that you want to mention?"

"You'll have to be specific," he smirked.

"Okay, fine," I said, thinking for a moment. "Do you play other instruments?"

"Yes."

"What's your favorite?

"Violin."

"What's your power?" I asked.

He paused for a moment. "I'd much rather hear about yours."

He certainly doesn't like to talk about himself. "I'm surprised you don't already know," I said. He finished the last of his food and looked at me, engaged in what I was about to say. "It's Mind Sight. And you're avoiding my question."

"Tell me, Sight, what do you think my power is?" he inquired.

I thought for a moment remembering how he moved the door earlier. "It has something to do with moving objects without touching them, right?" I offered.

"See, I don't even have to tell you," Kasius said, his deep eyes catching mine for a moment. My heart fluttered.

I looked away nervously. "Do you want me to clean up the dishes?"

Kasius smirked. "No," he said, shaking his head.

"Okay," I said, standing. I accidentally dropped the napkin that I had in my lap. Crouching down, I picked it up, brushing my fingers across the floor.

Hunter, he's got a piece of wood in his hands, he's sanding it, examining it, sanding it. He's looking at someone. He's smiling at them —

There was a buzzing sound in my ears. "Esmari? Esmari?" Kasius whispered. I opened my eyes. He was kneeling next to me. My head was spinning. He had a hand on my shoulder. "Hey, there you go."

"What—" I started to ask. My mind was in such a fog that I lost my sentence as soon as I began.

Kasius looked at me with concern in his eyes. Still, he smiled at me. "Why don't I walk you back to your dorm?" he asked, helping me up.

"I—I'm okay. Really," I reassured. "Thank you for dinner."

He smiled at me again, but didn't object as I headed on my own toward my dorm room. The sounds of the hall seemed muffled in my ears, almost like I was cupping my hands over my ears as I walked. I made it back to my dorm and felt groggy and tired. I felt like I was still in a haze. I reached up to my necklace, but it wasn't there.

"No!" I gasped.

I thought about heading down the hall to look for it, but exhaustion washed over me. My heart sank. Without the necklace in my hands, and my head as foggy as it was, I questioned for a moment if I was still in an episode. I sat on my bed and heard a crinkle in my pocket. Carefully, I pulled out the now wrinkled letter from Bray and tossed it onto the desk. I laid my head on my pillow and closed my eyes.

———

Late the next morning, I woke up to a tap on my door. I rubbed the sleep from my eyes and crawled myself out of bed. I thought back on the events of the previous day and smiled to myself at the diversity that the day had brought. I touched my neck, my fingers looking for my necklace, and then remembered. Frowning to myself, I twisted the cool doorknob and opened my door.

A small box sat at my feet. I looked around, only to see the halls empty. Shrugging, I picked up the box and opened it to find my necklace sitting on a folded note. I sighed with happiness at the sight of it, and embraced the flood of memories it brought back. I took it out and unfolded the note underneath.

Found this at my dorm. The clasp broke. Hope you don't mind that I replaced it for you. Let's just say it's something else I'm good at.

"Kasius," I sighed.

"What about him?" Jewel said, coming out of her dorm.

"Nothing," I said, shaking my head.

My phone rang inside my dorm. Tossing the box to the side, I answered it, Jewel trailing behind.

"Hello?"

"Es?" Hunter's voice asked.

"Hunter, what's going on?"

"Okay, you are not going to believe this. I had to call you and tell you first. Oh, this is just so cool!

"What is it?" I laughed.

"I got it! The apprenticeship! I got it! I am going to be a carpenter's apprentice! A paid one!" Hunter announced half yelling into the other end of the phone.

"That's great!" I exclaimed. Jewel looked at me, confused. I whispered to her, "he got the apprenticeship!"

Jewel jumped up and down with joy. "Yay, Hunter! Congrats!" she called out.

"Is that Jewel? Tell her thanks! Oh, and the guys and I are checking out a house today to maybe move into! It sounds promising. And if it works out, we could be moving in by next week! I tell you, Es! Things are going so great right now!"

"Hunter, we are so happy for you!"

"I gotta get off the phone, Finn needs to use it. Come by tomorrow night, we are going to have a gathering to celebrate! Bye!"

I hung up the phone and brushed through my hair. Jewel joined me at the mirror and played with her hair a bit.

"Are you planning on going to the academy today?" Jewel asked, finally deciding to put her hair in a messy ponytail.

I thought of Mr. Sean sobbing in the classroom the day before. "Yeah, I have a few things to do," I mentioned.

"Well, I'm free today. Can I join you? Maybe I can help with your studies. Plus, I'm bored," Jewel said with persuasion.

I smiled at her. *It would be nice to study with someone for once.* "You know what, yeah, that would be great," I told her.

"Yay! Oh, this is going to be fun! I've never been to the Sight classroom before. How interesting! And maybe I'll see the infamous Mr. Sean!" she rambled, her eyes twinkling with delight.

I shook my head at her and breathed out a soft chuckle. "Let's go."

We made our way to the academy. The weather today was completely opposite of the day before. It was sunny and warm, full of hope. The halls of the academy were full of life today, too, though the closer to the classroom we came, the quieter it became. Jewel stuck close to me. I could feel the conflicting emotions of excitement and fear rising in her. I smiled at her reassuringly. I had forgotten how spooky it was to be at the back of the school. I suppose I had just gotten used to it, but Jewel hadn't, yet. We entered the classroom and could hear a conversation flooding the room.

"Higgens, that's not how it works," Mr. Sean said.

"But you could learn, Sean. The elders are just concerned. It's been too quiet," Mr. Higgens said.

"I understand that, but I'm not a guard. And you know that there are limits to my abilities," Mr. Sean sighed with frustration.

I turned to Jewel and motioned for the door. "We should go," I whispered.

"Esmari! I know you're there!" Mr. Sean called. "I can see you, remember?"

I cringed at Jewel, and motioned for her to wait where she was. Stepping lightly, I went over to Mr. Higgens and Mr. Sean, who were standing just inside of his office.

"I'm sorry, we can come back later. I didn't mean to interrupt," I apologized. Mr. Higgens looked at me for a moment in thought, then back at Mr. Sean.

"Higgens, no," Mr. Sean shook his head.

"Okay, you've made yourself clear. Don't worry about it, Esmari, I am just heading back. Please, enjoy your studies." Mr. Higgens said, nodding toward me and making his exit.

I turned to Mr. Sean and looked him over briefly. He pinched the bridge of his nose for a moment and shook his head again. I gave him some time to relax.

"I brought along a friend to study with today," I said finally. He opened his eyes and looked at me. I expected anger in that moment, but his face was calm. He nodded and turned away.

Returning to Jewel, we got straight to studying. She mostly just watched or commented, asking an occasional question here or there. I told her some of the different things I had read recently about connections. She was determined to help me find some control over my power, so she came up with a game to try. We sat opposite of each other on the floor, her back to me. She would use water to form a shape in her hands, and I would have to use my Sight to guess it.

"I think, that because we are close friends, maybe if we play this game, you will be able to get somewhere with your control of your Mind Sight. If anything, it's worth a try," she said with hope.

"Okay," I agreed. "Sure, why not. Let's give it

a go."

"Great!" she said. She turned away from me, and I could see her shoulders moving as she formed the liquid in her hands. "What shape did I make?"

I closed my eyes and placed my tingling fingers on the ground. *A book, sitting open on the ground* – I opened my eyes and lifted my hand from the ground.

"That's not what I was trying to see," I whispered to myself with a pout.

Shaking my head, I brushed it off and tried again. Three more times, I tried. I had seen the podium, the door, and Jewel's hair, which seemed promising at first, but that was as far as that got. Irritated with myself, I fiddled with the necklace and stared up at the light hanging above us.

"Well?" Jewel asked.

"A ball," I said sarcastically.

"What? Yeah! It is!" she said, turning to me with excitement. "You did it!"

"No, I just guessed, I didn't see it," I sighed.

"Aw, I thought it actually worked. You're too upset. It's just a game, remember, Es? Relax. Let's try again," she said. She turned back around and giggled. "Okay, what shape?"

I smiled at her. It was just a game. She was

right. I thought about her hands and closed my eyes. Gently, I placed my palm on the floor and listened for Jewel's breathing. *She's moving her hands, keeping the water in shape, its —*

"A cube," I grinned, lifting my hand.

"Yes! I knew you could do it!" Jewel exclaimed, tossing her hands in the air. We watched the water splash onto the ground in front of her. "Oops."

I laughed. *I had actually seen what I was trying to for once.* "Let's try again!" I said eagerly.

Jewel grabbed at her rumbling stomach and glance at the clock. "Maybe after lunch?" she offered sheepishly.

We went to the cafeteria and grabbed our lunch. Sitting at an empty table, Jewel and I chatted about the success of the game. We thought of different ways to play it and how to make it more challenging as I increased my capability. I think she was just as excited about the progress as I was.

"My dad said that a part of him hopes the Ex was bluffing. But he still wants me to be careful being a possible target and all," Belleza told Lilly as they passed by our table. Jewel and I rolled our eyes.

"Did he really tell you that you're a target?" Lilly asked wide-eyed. They took a seat at a table across the way from us, which Kasius was already occupying.

"Well, not exactly. But the way he keeps telling me to be careful, I know," Belleza said with a shrug. "Kasius will protect me, though, won't you?"

Kasius looked up at Belleza as she bat her eyes at him. His cold expression never wavered. Lilly glanced between the two of them, eagerly awaiting his answer. He looked away and swiftly slid his chair back. Standing, he took the book he had and bowl of fruit and walked to our table. He didn't even hesitate. I could see Belleza behind him, her mouth wide open. Kasius looked at me with a gentle smile, then sat down in the seat next to me. I glanced up at Belleza, who was now glaring at me with fire in her eyes. Kasius opened his book back up and took a bite of fruit as if nothing had happened.

"Today is just full of surprises!" Jewel noted under her breath. She looked at me and nodded to Kasius with a sly smile. I shook my head at her and took a bite of my food.

I glanced again at Belleza's glaring eyes that felt as if they were trying to burn a hole in my forehead. They darted back and forth from Kasius to me. Trying not to laugh, I directed my attention back onto my plate of food.

"You know she's still glaring at us," I said to Kasius with a slight smirk.

"Mm-hm," Kasius nodded. He continued reading his book.

"Did I miss something?" Jewel asked.

"I thought you were hungry. You haven't even taken a bite yet," I teased.

She gave a sigh of defeat and shoved a big bite of burrito in her mouth. We ate our meal and chatted a bit more. Kasius read quietly beside me, occasionally turning the page. When he had finished his fruit, he stood and nodded a silent goodbye to the two of us before leaving the cafeteria.

sixteen

The following afternoon, Jewel and I got ready together. We wanted to dress up and make a special occasion out of the celebration for Hunter's new apprenticeship. We even made him a cake, which I secretly hoped would taste better then it looked. Jewel curled my hair and pinned it back for me. When she and I had decided we were satisfied with our looks, we collected the cake and made our way to Hunter's dorm, where we found everyone just inside of the lobby.

"Hey, Es!" Hunter greeted, waving at us as we entered. He came jogging over to us.

"Hey, Hunter. Congrats! We made a surprise for you!" I said.

Jewel and I held out the cake box for him. "Ta-da!" We said in unison, propping open the lid for him to see.

His face lit up with pure joy. "Yay Huntee?" He said, reading the top of the cake.

"Aw, man! The 'r' got smudged," Jewel frowned. "Welp, you are now Huntee, the carpentee's apprentice."

Hunter laughed for a moment and placed the lid back on the cake box. "Thanks! Oh, hey, Jewel, I have to introduce you to everyone," he said, leading us over to the group. "That's Moz, Darren, Finn, and this is Flow. Everyone, this is Jewel."

"How about I cut up this cake for us?" Jewel offered. Chimes of approval spread among the group.

Finn took out some paper plates from a nearby cabinet and helped her serve up the cake for everyone. Hunter and I took a seat. For a moment, I took in the happiness. I listened to the chatter among the small gathering. Moz and Darren were bickering with each other playfully. Jewel and Finn were jabbering away as they dished up. Flow was laughing with Moz and Darren at a joke she told them. Hunter was grinning away, having the time of his life.

"You excited?" I asked Hunter.

"Yeah! So excited. It's like a dream. I don't feel like it's quite real yet," he smiled. "Pinch me, will ya?"

I leaned over and pinched at his shoulder. "There," I said slyly.

"Ouch! Hey! I was kidding, you know," he said, whacking me with a pillow. He paused and turned to me, grabbing my shoulders and shaking me. "I am going to be an apprentice, Es. An apprentice! Ah!"

I grabbed his shoulders back. "I know!" I said, shaking him, too.

He fell back against the couch dramatically while holding my hand to his chest. "Who would have thought a tailor's kid would be good at carpentry?" he said with a dreamy sigh.

"You're a goofball," I laughed.

"Hey, drama queen, do you want some of your cake or not?" Finn teased, holding out a rather mangled slice of cake to each of us. Taking the plate from Finn, I glanced up to see Flow watching the entire encounter between Hunter and me. She looked down as if embarrassed and disappointed.

"So, how's it going with Flow?" I whispered, shoving a big bite of surprisingly delicious cake in my mouth.

"It, well, it's going. I think I'm going to ask her to coffee or something," Hunter said back, fidgeting with his fork like a child.

"You should!" I smiled. "Oh, yeah, did you guys get the house?"

"I totally forgot to tell you! We got it! We move in next week! It's so cool. Right on the edge of the West District. Lots of room and a great price range for rent. The guy who owns it is pretty cool too."

"Maybe we could show them after we finish the cake?" Finn offered.

"Yeah! That sounds like fun! Right, Es?" Jewel chimed.

After we had all finished our slices of cake, and Finn got done chasing Hunter around with a leftover glob of frosting, we headed outside. The boys led us as we flew to take a look at their new place. We arrived and hovered over it as they told us all kinds of details about it. The forest edge was just an empty field away and was peaceful to look at with its tall pine trees. They told us who planned to take which room and how they were going to turn the living area into a lounge area just like at the dorms. Hunter pointed out the building he was going to be working at, just a few streets away. He told me all about his plans and what he was hoping to learn about carpentry. I enjoyed listening to him just ramble away, explaining it all.

The sun began to set, leaving a warm orange glow over Banshui. Finn came over to join Hunter and me, throwing an arm around Hunter's shoulder. They joked back and forth with each other for a moment.

Finn looked slyly at Hunter. "Race ya!"

"I'm in!" called Moz.

"Esmari, you coming?" Hunter smiled.

"No way! She's too fast!" said Darren. "I want a fair race!"

"You go ahead," I laughed.

"Last one back does the dishes for a week!" Said Finn.

The guys all dashed after one another, grinning as they raced. Flow, Jewel, and I giggled and laughed at their competitive natures. I felt a warmth in my heart grow, watching Hunter enjoying his time with these friends of his. It made me smile, thinking about how happy he had been since we arrived in Banshui. A part of me almost felt he belong here more than I did. Like this was his true home, instead of mine.

"Esmari, you and Hunter seem pretty close,"

Flow said as she, Jewel, and I flew back toward the guys' dorm.

I looked at Jewel, knowing what Flow intended to ask, but was too shy to say. Jewel nudged me. "See, I'm not the only one who thinks it," Jewel teased.

"Yeah, he's my best friend. We practically grew up together," I smiled at Flow. Her smile fell slightly, and I could see a twinkle fading from her eyes. "Flow, Hunter really likes you, you know."

"Really?" she breathed with a tinge of embarrassment.

"Yeah, really. Trust me when I say, there's nothing between us but a long-standing friendship. I can tell you like him back. I won't stand in your way, ever," I said to her. She blushed slightly in the fading light.

———

The following week, Hunter and his friends had settled into their new home. Moz, who had lost the race back to the dorm, had also lost a second race the next day, leading to not one, but two weeks of dishes on his end. All of which Hunter bragged about on the phone with me from his new place.

"You should've seen his face!" He laughed.

"He really should stop betting with you guys. He always seems to lose," I noted.

"How's your studying going? Jewel told me that you two had come up with a neat game to play that seems to be working."

"Yeah, I feel like it has really helped progress my control."

"Well, you two will have to show me next time you're over. I gotta go. Finn needs me to help him build a shelf. Talk to you soon, Es!"

"Bye, Hunter."

I hung up the phone as a chill ran down my spine. Something in the air felt different today, and I just couldn't shake the feeling of uneasiness it gave me. Jewel came in my open door behind me.

"You ready?" she asked, still clasping a necklace around her neck.

I took one last look in the mirror. Tugging down my charcoal gray t-shirt into place, I nodded. I quickly knelt down and tied up my shoes. A tingling sensation ran all the way up my arms into my shoulders. I sighed and touched the floor giving in to my power for a moment. *Hunter and Finn are laughing. Tossing things at each other as they work on the shelf. Hunter's hazel eyes are smiling. A tuff of his jet-black hair is dangling out of place –* My surroundings came back. I took a breath and touched my necklace, getting my stability back.

"The urge is stronger, isn't it?" Jewel asked in a hushed tone.

"Yeah, it's okay, though," I shrugged off.

We headed to the academy together. There was a slight breeze that accompanied us as we walked. It was warm out, and the sun was already beaming down from high in the sky. Jewel was chatting away about what she was learning recently in class, but I found it hard to focus on the conversation. We entered through the doors of the academy, our heels clicking against the echoing floors. I waved her goodbye and started toward my class. My mind wandered on what lessons and exercises I wanted to work on for the day.

It was quiet in the classroom when I entered. Mr. Sean was sitting against the wall, reading through a book and taking notes on a small paper on the ground next to him. He didn't even look up at me. *He seems as distracted as I am.* I smiled to myself, ready to occupy myself in my studies.

I found a book that seemed interesting. It was a hand-written journal filled with all sorts of information on different Sights, but mainly about the writer's experience with their own Sight. The writing in it was faded on some pages and was written with different terminology, making me think it was written a long time ago. As I read on, the sensation of my power danced in my veins. It was bothersome. I kept trying to focus on my book.

BANG!

"Arg!" Mr. Sean grunted.

I glanced up to see a pile of books scattered on the floor. He collected them one by one and returned them to the shelf they had fallen from, muttering as he went. He picked up one and paused on it, turning it over a few times in his hands.

"Well, that's where you ended up," he mumbled to himself. Carefully, he thumbed through its pages, which seemed weathered and worn from use.

A now nagging ache lay dormant in my shoulders and neck. It was more of a nuisance than it had ever felt before. I found myself clenching my jaw as I stared just in front of me at the floor.

"What?" Mr. Sean asked.

I couldn't take the sickening sensation anymore. "Gah! Fine!" I yelled at my power.

I closed the book up and tossed it to the side and slammed both hands onto the floor before me. Instantly, everything went blank. I was looking over top of somewhere. A building, no, a house. It was familiar. *Something doesn't feel right. It's Hunter's house, maybe?* My surroundings came back to me. I felt confused. My power felt unsatisfied.

"I don't understand!" I cried.

"Esmari?" Mr. Sean asked.

I ignored him. I didn't want to answer. I couldn't answer. Another surge washed over me, it felt like static electricity in my arms. I took a look at my palms for a moment, then slammed them back down on the brick flooring. Everything went blank again. It was Hunter's house for sure this time. *There's a person. A male. His back is to me. He's standing outside. Just standing. Waiting. He's looking up to the sky for something. I can see Hunter pass by the window. He's looking back at someone inside. He's laughing. He doesn't see the man outside. The man is raising his hands. He's turned now. His face is lit up. It's scruffy, dirty. His cheeks are gaunt. Something is glowing in his hands. Fire? He's smiling. He's throwing something at the house. The house is on fire. There's an explosion –*

My surroundings came back to me, but everything still felt like a fog. My heart was pounding in my ears, which still were ringing from the sound of the explosion I had heard. I shook my head. It felt like a balloon.

"Esmari?" Mr. Sean said. I could see his shoes

just to the side of me. His trench coat was draped over his knees as he knelt.

"No," I muttered. "No, no, no."

"Esmari?" Mr. Sean said again. His voice was soft and laced with concern.

"No, that didn't happen," I muttered. I still couldn't shake the fog from my head. Everything felt muddled.

"What didn't? What did you see?" Mr. Sean demanded softly. I could tell he was growing worried.

I just kept shaking my head. The explosion boomed in my mind again. I covered my ears, squishing my palms firmly against them as if trying to squeeze out any noises. The man's face came into my mind again. Terror and anger grew inside of me. I grabbed for my necklace, finally. I felt its stone against my fingertips. Tears streamed down my cheeks. Hunter's face flashed in my mind.

"Hunter!" I gasped.

I scrambled to get up. Barging out of the classroom, I raced down the hall. My feet pounding against the floor as I wound through the winding hallways. I pushed past someone in the lobby, Kasius, maybe. I didn't care. I flung open the entry doors, my heart still pounding in my chest. Someone was behind me, following me. I didn't look back. I couldn't think. I took off, flying up into the sky. I flew as fast as I could in the direction of Hunter's house, in the direction of the smoke. I could hear someone's wings flapping an uneven rhythm somewhere in the growing distance behind me. As I grew closer, a gaping hole in my chest formed. *Faster, Esmari, faster!* I focused in on the direction I needed to go, dodging around trees and other people. The smell of dirt and smoke filled the air making it hard to breathe. I didn't care.

I landed and took a look around. I squinted through the haze, walking carefully as I went. My foot stepped on something. It crunched. I looked down to see broken glass and brick and roof tiles scattered about. My mind raced. Then I saw it. The house, now a pile of rubble.

seventeen

My breath caught in my throat. I wasn't sure if it was from the shock of it all or the smoky haze surrounding me. Maybe a little bit of both. I scanned the area for any sign of Hunter. For any sign of anyone. A shift in the settling rubble made my heart skip.

"Hunter?" I called, my voice cracking. "Hunter!"

There was no answer. I thought back to what I had seen. Hunter was in the house. Maybe someone else, too. Hot tears flooded my eyes.

"Hunter!" I cried out again.

Still nothing. I began to mindlessly dig into the rubble now at my feet. I yanked at each piece of tile, each piece of wood, chucking it behind me. Sweat dripped down my neck. I wiped my eyes on my sleeve and continued. Digging and digging and digging. *Hunter, where are you?* My fingers ached. The more I dug, the less I felt like I was getting anywhere.

"Hunter!" I cried out again. "Say something, Hunter!"

I couldn't think of what else to do, I just kept digging and crying. My heart ached. My head was spinning. Movement from the corner of my eye made my heart flutter.

"Hunter!" I called out to the figure hidden in smoke.

I couldn't tell who they were. I listened for an answer. Any indication that it was Hunter. I wanted to hear his voice more than I wanted breath in my lungs.

"Hunter!" I called again. The figure stepped closer to me. It wasn't him.

"Es?" Said the voice. I squinted through the haze. Finn was staggering toward me. "Es!"

"Finn, where's Hunter?" I pleaded.

"I don't know. I just remember seeing a flash

of something over near the kitchen. Hunter shoved me away. I don't know what happened after that," Finn said, squeezing his eyes shut. He had blood smeared down his cheek from a gash on his head. He was holding a limp arm.

"Esmari!" called a voice behind me.

I turned to see Mr. Sean looking at me through the settling haze. He caught sight of a barely stable Finn and rushed to his side. Walking carefully, he guided Finn away from the rubble and sat him down. He pulled a cloth from his pocket and pressed it firmly against the gash on Finn's temple. I turned away and scanned the more visible surface of the rubble.

"Esmari!" called Mr. Sean. I didn't listen. I didn't want to know what he had to say to me.

"Hunter!" I screamed again, my voice growing hoarse. "Hunter! Say something!"

This didn't feel real. It was like a bad dream. Hunter, my best friend, wasn't answering. I wanted to find him. I *needed* to find him. My chest burned. My face was still wet with a never-ending stream of tears. I felt confused and lost. Standing up, I looked around again. That's when I saw it. A hand.

"Hunter!" I screamed.

My heart was racing. I crawled over the piles of rubble to Hunter. I cleared brick and glass from around him. His breathing was shallow. He was fighting it. I smoothed the hair from his forehead and wiped a smudge of dirt from his cheek.

"Hunter," I sobbed.

"Es?" he asked. His eyes were barely open.

"Yeah, Hunter, it's me. It's Es."

"Es, I don't feel right."

"I know. Shh," I hushed. "It's okay."

I looked around, trying to see through the haze. *Where was Mr. Sean now? When I needed him!* I couldn't see a thing. Hunter's labored breathing made my stomach tie in knots. *How was I going to get him out of here?* I looked down at his blood-stained shirt. *I don't know what to do. I don't know how to help him! Please!*

"Help!" I screamed. "Somebody!"

"I'm cold," Hunter whispered.

"Okay, I've got you," I said, rubbing at his arms.

I looked around again, frantically. I couldn't see anyone. My heart pounded in my chest. Hunter winced as some of the rubble settled under him. I put pressure against where the gash was on his side. *Why isn't anyone here to help me!*

"Hey Es?" Hunter said, his voice growing softer.

"Yeah, Hunter?"

"I like Banshui, can we stay?" he asked as he reached for my hand.

I smiled softly and wrapped my hands around his. "Yeah, Hunter. We can stay." I said with a wavering voice. His eyes closed and his hand went limp in mine. "No, Hunter! Hunter! Stay with me, Hunter."

I searched his face for movement. Any sign that he was okay. It felt like a sick joke. I wanted it to be a sick joke. I wanted him to open his eyes up and say "gotcha" with that sly look of his. I pressed his hand to my chest, feeling my entire world come crashing down and wailed out from somewhere within. My chest hurt.

The man's face flashed in my head. Suddenly, I grew angry. My hands trembled with rage. I wanted to find him. I wanted him to pay. I stood and found my way to a clear patch of grass. There was a fire creeping up my throat. I was going to find him.

"Ah!" I yelled with infuriation.

Dropping to my knees, I dug my hands into the half-burnt grass with one intention in mind. I shut my eyes and focused on the man. I felt a surge of energy in my fingers as everything faded. *Where are you!* I saw a figure; his scruffy features were undeniable. *There you are.* He was beginning to try to hover. He was nearby. I didn't want him to get away. I thought about grabbing hold of him. Yanking him back onto the ground. Throwing him down. And then it happened. I don't exactly know how, but it happened.

I opened my eyes. I didn't have time to question it. Quickly, I flew up and darted to him, lying still on the ground. He rolled over to face me. I glared at his gaunt face, anger raging through my veins. I lifted my hand and felt an energy around my fist like I had never felt before. This energy, this power, surged through my arms, and I could feel it in my wings. There was a glow around me. The man's eyes widened as he looked at me, glistening with the reflection of flickering colors. I raised up my arm, ready to attack the man.

"Do it," whispered a voice.

I couldn't tell where it was coming from. I shook my head. Conflicted with emotions. I looked in his face. Again, I lifted my hand.

"He deserves it," said the voice again.

It was like a hissing in my ear.

"Do it," demanded the voice.

"Ah!" I yelled out, throwing what I could only describe as a swirling, sparking ball of white-purple lightning at the man.

He ducked to one side, and it left a charred mark in the grass where his head once was. Again, and again I shot at him, each time with a slightly different hue of the sparking ball coming from my hands. I wanted revenge. I wanted him to pay for what he did. I wanted him to feel the fear that Hunter felt. I wanted him to die like Hunter died. My veins throbbed with each surging blow I threw in his direction.

"Esmari!" Mr. Sean yelled. "Stop!"

He grabbed my wrist just as I was certain I would have gotten the man. Gently, he turned me to face him.

"Stop," he whispered.

He wasn't angry with me. There was pity and sorrow in his eyes as he pleaded with me. He carefully released my wrist and placed his hands on my trembling shoulders.

"Stop," he whispered again.

My heart pounded in my ears. I was angry and scared. *Why had he stopped me?* I didn't want him here.

"Aw, now come on, it was just getting good," Sneered the voice, now closer than before.

I looked to see a man. He turned his head slightly, and I caught sight of a small scar running along his jawline. He was tall and well dressed. He seemed familiar. It hit me. *The man from the shoe store in Sky Athra.* Mr. Sean stepped in front of me, placing himself between the two of us.

"Well, hi, Dad." The man's smile made my skin crawl. "It's really been a while, hasn't it?"

I glanced at Mr. Sean. He stared directly at the

man. His jaw was clenched with anger and determination. But his eyes showed a glimpse of sadness and disappointment.

The man smirked and continued. "Have you talked to mom lately? I hear her new hubby is really something."

"Why are you here, Byrein?" Mr. Sean snapped.

"What, no hello?" Byrein said with a fake pout. He dropped the pout and curled the corners of his lips, looking directly at me. "I'm here for her. She has quite the potential, if I do say so myself. Mind Sight, am I right?"

He stepped to the side to look at me better. Mr. Sean kept an arm out in front of me as if to protect me.

"Shame, about your friend, I mean. I only wanted him to scare them. Just enough to get your blood pumping. To draw you out. I wanted to see if I was right about you being the one. And was I ever! Though you really, honestly, exceeded my expectations. You see, I wanted to see if we could, shall we say, kick start your power. Put it into high gear, so to speak. It was taking much too long for you to progress on your own. This guy seemed to get a little carried away, though. Ah, oh, well. It worked nonetheless." Byrein said, peering down at the man now cowering on the ground.

"What do you want with me?" I asked.

"If I told you, it wouldn't be as much fun, now, would it!" Byrein said, his cold black eyes hungry for entertainment.

I stared in disbelief. *Fun?*

"Ah, well, fine. There are certain—" He paused thinking for a moment. "Certain doors, that open up when you have a strong Royal, but to have more than one strong Royal involved, and to have two Mind Sights—" He sucked in a slow breath reveling in the thought.

"You can't have her," Mr. Sean breathed.

"You really haven't changed, have you, Dad?" Byrein smirked. "Still thinking that you can tell me what I can and cannot have."

"Enough," Mr. Sean sneered.

"Why don't we let the lady decide for herself," he said, softly licking the corner of his lips. His slick black feathered wings on his back flicked with excitement. "I expected greatness out of you, but I didn't expect you to be a Mixer."

I looked between Mr. Sean and Byrein. My heart now raced in my chest with terror. I furrowed my eyebrows at Byrein, not really knowing how to put what I was feeling into words.

"I know your answer. I know you aren't coming with me. Not today, at least," he sighed.

"Not ever," Mr. Sean hissed.

Byrein looked me directly in the eyes this time. A sharp pain engulfed my skull. *I will have you.* His voice boomed inside my head. *I need you, you'll see. You'll see that you need me, too.*

Mr. Sean looked between Byrein and me frantically. "Stop, Byrein!" Mr. Sean demanded. The pain stopped, and he took away his gaze. I felt vulnerable and empty inside.

"There is so much I can teach you. When you are ready, I will be more than willing to expand your knowledge. I can help expand your power in ways you can't even imagine. You have so much more potential than what Banshui has to offer to you, Esmari," Byrein said in a trance, his eyes glossed over as he seemingly stared directly into my soul.

"Havin' more power is not always good, Byrein," Mr. Sean said.

"See, that's what the difference is between you and me, Dad. You were always content just as you were. You didn't want change, you never have. Well, change is progress. And I wanted progress. I wanted to be better, and you always wanted to hold me back!" Byrein hissed.

He gazed off into the distance for a moment. His eyes glossing over. He blinked a few times and looked back at us with a smile. "Well, they certainly took long enough. And, that's my cue to leave. I will bid you farewell here," he said with a small bow. He looked directly at my eyes. "Until next time."

The man on the ground scrambled to get up. He flashed a creepy smile as if to taunt us. Walking backward, he began to fly up into the air and took off toward the forest. Byrein turned to follow him. He had just begun to hover when he stopped and dropped back to the ground. He glanced over his shoulder at us.

"It's unusual to see you care about anyone, Dad," he sneered. "Who even is she to you?"

"She's my student," Mr. Sean said without hesitation.

"After me, they still let you teach students?" He chuckled. "I'm surprised."

Byrein ticked his tongue. He took one last look at me with his piercing black eyes as if to imprint a picture of my face in his mind. Then, he took off into the sky just as a couple of people wearing elaborately embroidered coats joined us. I noticed the faint glisten of the letters "ORP" down the arm of one of the women's coat. One began examining the area, while another took off after the small speck that once was Byrein.

My hands were trembling, and my knees became wobbly. I collapsed to the ground in shock of everything. I didn't understand. I felt lost. Confused. Scared. *Byrein really did all of this just because he wanted me?* Hot tears trickled down my cheeks. I had felt like just days ago, I was beginning to find my feet underneath me. I thought I was finally understanding my place here in Banshui. And now, today, everything came crashing down again. I looked down at my hands that felt foreign to me. The palms were blotchy and puffy and covered in Hunter's dried blood. I wanted more than anything to understand what had happened to me.

Mr. Sean crouched beside me. "Did you know?" He asked softly with his raspy voice.

"What?"

"That your abilities went beyond Mind Sight. Did you know?" He asked again.

My lip quivered, and I shook my head. I had no idea what had even happened. I looked at him, searching his face for answers. I peered once again down at my hands. A thought of the sparking ball sitting in my hands flashed across my mind. I shut my eyes tight and drew in a sharp breath. *What had I done?*

"Mr. Sean. What did I do? Who am I

becoming?" I sobbed.

"Esmari," Mr. Sean sighed with a crack in his voice. "I don't know."

I sat in the grass, sobbing. I don't even know for how long. Mr. Sean sat beside me. He said nothing, I don't think he knew what to say to me. The entire world seemed to stop.

I knew there were people now behind me, digging in the rubble. I didn't turn to acknowledge them. I was terrified of myself. I was terrified of my power that was growing within me. The power that I apparently have coursing through my veins. I wanted so badly to wake up from my nightmare.

I let my mind float over the events of the past several months. *What had gotten me here? What had gotten me to this point?* I had more questions than I had answers now. I questioned everything about myself. I no longer knew up from down, it seemed.

Byrein wanted me. The whole time. It was me he wanted. Not Belleza. Not a solid crown Royal. Me. I didn't understand what he wanted me for. It scared me that not even Mr. Sean seemed to understand fully. What scared me more was Byrein seemed to know more about me than I knew about myself.

"Is Byrein a Mind Sight, like me?" I asked with a crack in my voice.

Mr. Sean looked at me solemnly, and slowly

nodded. "Yes."

I mulled over that thought in my head. He had answers that no one else could give me. Yet, he was the last person I wanted to hear those answers from. I felt more alone than I had ever felt. My chest ached with sadness. My arms and shoulders shook from exhaustion. I had lost what I knew as my identity. I didn't recognize the power surging in my veins. My rage drove me to nearly kill a man. And most importantly, I had lost my best friend.

I finally found the strength to pull myself up off the ground. I paused for a moment, touching my fingertips out of habit to my necklace resting on my neck. Mr. Sean stood next to me, his hands shoved deep in his trench coat pockets, just as they always seemed to be. He winced as his wings twitched on his back, the scarred wing looking even worse off than before. Patiently, he waited next to me. When I had finally stabilized myself, I took a step. And then another. Mindlessly, I walked toward the rubble, toward Hunter.

Maya and Corbin were there. I could see tears glistening on both of their cheeks. Corbin held Maya's shoulders to comfort her. When I came closer, she looked at me in the eyes. She didn't speak, but her sorrowful eyes kept apologizing over and over. I looked down on the ground in the grass to where someone had laid Hunter's body. It was odd to see him so quiet and calm.

I wanted him to get up and joke with me one last time. I wanted him to gush over my mom's muffins. I wanted him to tell me all about his carpentry work. I needed him to smile at me with that goofy grin he always had. I needed him to call my name. To laugh with me. To sit up. To move. To breathe. To live.

He just laid there motionless, covered in filth.

Hunter, your hair is a mess. I've never seen you to be so careless about your looks. And there's dirt on your face, you know. Your shirt's ripped, too. I wonder if you will fix it like your dad taught you how. The air feels like that day in Athra, do you remember? When we sat and ate ice cream, and people watched, playing that game we used to play. The one you always won. Let's play that again. You just need to get up. Please, Hunter. Get up.

"Please, Hunter," I sobbed, kneeling next to him. "You have to get up."

I closed my eyes and cried. The sun's warmth began to cool by the time my tears dried up. I didn't want to move. Maya, Corbin, and Mr. Sean didn't leave me. They stayed with me, without a word. They never asked me to get up. They never came over to me. They let me sit there the entire afternoon. I was numb.

There comes a day in every person's life when they come of age. They grow up. They receive their wings. I used to think it was some special time. That when that day came, I would feel empowered, mature. I thought I'd feel complete. Everything would change. Life would be everything that I would hope for and more. I thought that life would make sense. That having wings would make my life easier. Yet, as I sat in the grass holding Hunter's lifeless head in my lap that afternoon, I realize how very wrong I was about all of it. All except one thing. Everything changed, just not in the way I was hoping for. I lost everything I ever knew and loved the day I got my wings.